The Wondrous Woo

The Wondrous Woo

a novel by

Carrianne K. Y. Leung

inanna poetry & fiction series

INANNA PUBLICATIONS AND EDUCATION INC.
TORONTO, CANADA

Canada Council **Conseil des Arts**
for the Arts du Canada

 **ONTARIO ARTS COUNCIL**
CONSEIL DES ARTS DE L'ONTARIO

We gratefully acknowledge the support of the Canada Council for the Arts and the Ontario Arts Council for our publishing program. We also acknowledge the financial support of the Ontario Media Development Organization.

We are also grateful for the support received from an
Anonymous Fund at The Calgary Foundation.

Note from the publisher: Care has been taken to trace the ownership of copyright material used in this book. The author and the publisher welcome any information enabling them to rectify any references or credits in subsequent editions.

Cover artwork: Alexander Barattin

Library and Archives Canada Cataloguing in Publication

Leung, Carrianne K. Y., author
    The wondrous Woo / Carrianne K.Y. Leung.

(Inanna poetry and fiction series)
Issued in print and electronic formats.
ISBN 978-1-77133-068-8 (pbk.) — ISBN 978-1-77133-071-8 (pdf)

    I. Title. II. Series: Inanna poetry and fiction series

PS8623.E9353W66 2013   C813'.6   C2013-905393-X
                                            C2013-905394-8

Printed and bound in Canada

 MIX
Paper from
responsible sources
FSC **FSC® C004071**

Inanna Publications and Education Inc.
210 Founders College, York University
4700 Keele Street, Toronto, Ontario, Canada M3J 1P3
Telephone: (416) 736-5356 Fax: (416) 736-5765
Email: inanna.publications@inanna.ca   Website: www.inanna.ca

To my Pau Pau,
who was the first writer.

Chapter 1 ⚏

APART FROM *KUNG FU* FILMS and Chinese New Year, everything our Ba had wanted for us was Canadian. He liked to say he was *gung-ho* for Canada, *gung-ho* being a word he used every chance he got. It sounded almost Chinese, he said.

When we first moved to Scarborough from Hong Kong in the late 1970s, Ba had enrolled us in skating classes and skiing lessons, let us eat grilled cheese and renamed us with English names, names with intention, names destined for big things. Sophia's was after the luscious screen siren Sophia Loren; Darwin's came from Charles Darwin; and, I got Miramar, which meant "view of the sea" and was the name of a town in Mexico where Ba's colleague had come from. Initially, my parents had not been able to get the consonants right, saying *Mi-La-Ma*, but Ba had loved it and laboured for months to pronounce it properly, reading the newspaper aloud at night to practice the "r"s. It was a glamorous name meant for a glamorous person. I wanted to live up to it, for Ba, though the older I got, the more it would be impossible to even try.

Ba had worked hard to instill the great Canadian mythology in the family so we would be as *gung-ho* as he was. Of course, once we had arrived in our new country, we realized that the mythology was not so great. There had not been any lumberjacks felling trees on our street, or Mounties guiding their horses among the strip malls. But Ba had been undeterred. Once we had settled into our suburban subdivision with its cookie-cutter semi-detached houses and young trees, Ba invited all the neighbours over for a barbeque to make sure we would have some friends right away.

Ma, who had not said much since we had arrived in our adopted country, had set her lips hard and went to work at cooking, making the kitchen come alive to the sound of banging pots and pans. Ma had not been as *gung-ho* about *Ka-La-Dai* as Ba. The rest of us had caught on pretty quickly, inserting the "eh" when appropriate and taking up the Canadian accent. Ma never even tried and had kept on speaking in Cantonese to us as much as possible so we would not forget. The language stayed the same, but she was not the same Ma she had been in Hong Kong. She never complained, but she had become quieter. Like all of us, I'd figured she just had to adjust.

But Ba, a wide grin on his face, standing there in his plaid Bermuda shorts, a neon-coloured polo shirt, and his fishing hat on his head as he grilled white fish and slapped the men on the shoulders while they talked, had seemed completely at home.

Standing in our yard, our neighbours had been nervous, we could tell, by the food, by how different we were. They had poked at the pork marinated in red sauce, skewered squid and fish balls, and salad mixed in a whole jar of mayonnaise. They had nodded and smiled and were extremely polite. "Is there plumbing in China? What's it like to live with communism? Is Hong Kong where all the toys are made?"

We kids had debriefed afterward, examining these *gweilos*, or foreigners, as if they were lab rats. Some *gweilos* were hairy, even some of the women. The children were grass-smeared, ketchup-faced, and jumpy as monkeys, but their parents had not seemed to mind. The grown-ups had enjoyed talk about chirpy things: the weather, insecticide for the lawns, their cars. At one point, Ba had mentioned Pierre Trudeau, our hero, but everyone clammed up, so he switched to the weather again and they had all relaxed.

In fairness, they had attempted to accept us; the women invited Ma to their coupon-clipping coffee meetings, and the men gave advice to Ba about eavestroughs. For the kids there had been much more mutual scrutiny. Fortunately, for Sophia, she was born two-finger whistle gorgeous, with long glossy hair and a heart-shaped face, even with her one wayward eye that refused to straighten despite all of Ma's efforts to train it when she was a baby by moving lollipops back and forth. Sophia had carried herself with the air of her namesake, and the girls gravitated to her with unabashed love. Little Darwin was hyper and loved to run and jump; the boys did not seem to be as particular about who they rode bikes with, so Darwin had fit right in.

As for me, I had never talked much, was thick like the trunk of a tree, and wore glasses that rose up my forehead and half-way down my cheeks. In my secret heart, I had hoped to live up to the breezy whispers of my name by dreaming of ocean panoramas, warm suns, and pretending I was someone else. I had stood off to the side, felt the heavy rim of mayonnaise in my mouth, and watched the scene alone, telling myself I did not mind.

Once Ba had found out about Disney World, he believed that pilgrimaging to the epicentre of the American dream would signal to the world that our little immigrant family had finally arrived. When he presented the idea to us, Sophia was in Grade 10, I was in Grade 13, and Darwin, though he looked seven, was deep into being eleven and far more into the violent acts he made his *Star Wars* action figures commit against other than twirling around in a boat amid dimpled dolls singing about what a small, small world it was.

But Ba had been oblivious to all of that. When he dumped the brochures out of his cracked leather briefcase onto the kitchen table, he had a smile that took up half his face. Ma had paused at her cooking and wiped her hands on her thighs before peering over his shoulder. "Wah! Florida? They don't need Florida. What? You think money grows on trees?" Ma had sniffed.

"C'mon, Ma. We've never taken them to Disney World, *la*. They deserve it," Ba had chided.

"Hrmph," Ma had turned back to the stove. She was not going to give in that easily.

Sophia and I had stared at the pictures of Snow White in front of her castle. Sophia just flicked her perfect hair behind her shoulder and stuck her nose in the air. I had tried to imagine us at Disney World together. Ma in her giant sun hat, Ba in his sports socks and sandals, the sullen teenage daughters, and the hyperactive son — me the slightly overweight nerd in too-tight Levis; Sophia, the cross-eyed beauty bored out of her blow-dried mind; and, little Darwin dwarfed by his too large second-hand Jedi Knight robes that he only took off to go to school and only after he did after his daily eight-fifteen a.m. tussle with Ma.

"What's for dinner?" Darwin had come flying into the kitchen, light saber in hand.

"Dar, we're going to Dis-Nee!" Ba had exclaimed as he tried to wrap his arm around Ma's waist while she shoved past him to return to her cooking.

"Disney?" Darwin had looked skeptically at the wide-eyed Mickey Mouse brochure. "That's for babies. Unless Disney made Darth Vader?"

"I don't think Disney made *Star Wars*," Sophia had said in her know-it-all voice. "They're more into the animals — Dumbo, Bambi. And the princesses. Snow White, Cinderella, Sleeping Beauty."

"Then forget it. I don't want to go to some baby place!" He had dropped the photo of Mickey Mouse back on the pile and ran out. "Call me when dinner's ready, Ma!"

Ba's smile had fallen like a landslide. "What about you girls? You used to love the princesses."

He looked like he had been trampled on.

He turned to me, his eldest, his rock, for support. "Miramar? You, too?" he asked quietly.

"Well, yeah, Ba. We're too old for that stuff." I had mumbled, resenting that I had to be the one to say it.

"Ah, okay. I made a mistake," Ba had said tunelessly as he swept the colourful brochures into his bag. "Only that so many of our neighbours have gone with their families. The travel agent said it's the great Canadian getaway."

Ma had already turned back to her pots on the stove and was stirring in silence. Ba then clicked his briefcase closed and went upstairs to change. We never talked about it again.

A few months after that, he was dead.

Chapter 2 〜

These fields will be yours one day, the father said. What good were fields, his irreverent children scowled. The girls were more interested in adorning their hair with jewelled combs while the son wanted to join his friends in chasing prized crickets. The father waited, knowing patience was the plight of the wise.

BA AND I USED TO HAVE this Sunday ritual of making the long hike downtown Toronto to the Golden Harvest theatre in Chinatown where we could take in the *kung fu* triple feature. Ba had a herniated disc from when he was young, so he lived vicariously through the *kung fu* masters as they exacted revenge on evildoers or those who had transgressed against their families. Ma didn't like the fighting, she said, and Darwin and Sophia hated all the standing at bus stops and crowded subway cars, so it was always just me and Ba, surrounded in the dark by grannies cracking pumpkin seeds with their teeth and the scents of roast duck and oranges wafting out of Tupperware containers.

Initially, I had gone with Ba just to keep him company, but as we watched the heroes move from happy innocence to tragedy to the final victory, I got hooked. Soon, I could hardly wait through the opening: the jaunty music, the debonair young men, the giggling peasant girls, everyone enjoying a happy-go-lucky life in their close-knit village with fertile fields and clear skies. This part had always seemed stupid to me, artificial. It was just like Scarborough. I would feel the sourness in my stomach when I thought about the *gweilo* kids at school, the same ones who had come to our summer BBQs and eaten our food, who in the halls, chanted "chinky-chong" taunts just loud enough for us to hear. That one girl who had gone around the cafeteria imitating Ma's herky-jerky shovelling motions while her fingers squished her eyes into slants.

But then, once the movie got going, I could not help but sit on the edge of my seat. This was when the warlords, the greedy landowners or corrupt government officials stripped the young protagonist of everything — his village, his family, his livelihood. As the sole survivor, he would receive training from the *kung fu* master, the old *sifu*, and eventually become the greatest warrior who ever lived, taking his revenge in incredible fight sequences and returning home victorious.

That part had made me feel as if I could leap through the screen with the grace of these heroes and kick some serious ass. When the credits rolled, Ba and I had always applauded.

While all the glory in these films belonged to the men, after a while, I had started noticing the women. They were usually on the periphery: the servant girls, the blind princesses, the poor orphans, the unwilling brides. Sometimes, the beautiful maidens' function was just to be beautiful, and they often ended up dead. But once in a while, when one of the women swept her long tresses aside and flew through the air, my heart would stop.

At night, I had only needed to close my eyes and I would inhabit their world, their quiet power. I imagined myself porcelain-skinned, clothed in layers of bright silk garments, feigning shyness by hiding behind a fan. The next moment, I yelled a battle cry and pointed to an opponent for offending my dignity. In a complex dance, we locked arms and battled to the death. I was always the victor, winning the awe and respect of the entire village, including the other top *kung fu* hero, the most handsome man of the bunch, the one whose sweat glistened as it dripped down his brown neck. Together, we travelled tirelessly, hunting the bad guys, avenging the innocent and saving the world.

When I was in Grade 11, we got our first VCR. Ba and I had stopped going to the Golden Harvest because even we had to admit it was far easier to stay home in our sweatpants than to spend all that time going downtown, especially since Ba had to make that commute every day for work anyway. But Sunday afternoons had remained our time; during the week he would pick up armloads of Hong Kong videos from a store on Spadina Avenue, and we would camp out all afternoon. When Sophia had whined that we were cutting into her shows, Ba bought another TV for the basement.

One afternoon by the third movie, I got annoyed. "These women are getting shafted," I had said, pointing to the eye-batting peasant girl washing clothes in the brook. "If she hadn't rescued her man from drowning, the show'd be over."

Ba had leaned over and paused the video, something we never did (we never needed to; peeing could always wait). He had scratched at his chin and looked me in the eye. "One day, Miramar," he said, "you should write these stories from the side of the women. Make the world know how powerful they are. Like you."

I had been mortified when my eyes welled up. Ba could always see through me even as I had tried to hide from myself. I had lived my *gung-ho* Canadian life in a timid shell. I had found shelter in the safety of our house, tucked my dreams inside these movies, and wished I were relevant while I hid in the shadows of my life. I had liked believing that deep within I was capable of everything I wanted, but at the same time, I had no idea how to be that person.

I thought I still had time to figure it all out. I thought there would be years of Ba in his La-z-Boy, me on the carpet, our hands balled up in fists during the fight sequences and thundering drumbeats, cheering loudly and high-fiving each other when the hero ultimately triumphed. I had thought Ba would always be around to help me find out who I was supposed to be. I was wrong.

Chapter 3 ⌒

After the screams subsided, and only the burning houses were left, Ye still crouched in her hiding place behind the rocks. She knew she had to get up and look for survivors, but still she waited, hoping for a sign — divine or otherwise. One by one, they came out of the shadows, their whispers growing louder as they groped for one another.

THE DAY HE DIED, I had just finished my last ever high-school exam and was celebrating being part of the graduating class of 1987 at McDonald's with my best friend, Nida.

"Yeah, but using tampons means you're not a virgin anymore," Nida asserted, using her best authoritative voice. She dipped a french fry gingerly into a pool of ketchup.

"You know jack shit," I mumbled with my mouth full of quarter pounder and cheese.

"Jack shit? What kind of shit is 'jack shit'?" Nida waved the red-tipped fry at me. We liked to swear like truck drivers when we were together. It made us feel dangerous.

Though I had used exactly three tampons in my life and not very well, I persevered in my impassioned defense. "You insert it, and you forget about it. Well, you don't forget about it. You know what I mean. You just don't have that big brick between your legs all day. You can run around, do things, even go swimming. And who cares if you're no longer a virgin. That's good. Then it won't hurt the first time."

"Ew. That's so gross. Anyway, my mother would freak if she

saw tampons in the house!" We both cackled at the thought of
Mrs. Patel coming across a box of tampons. She would likely
bang down the basement steps, slide open the storage closet
doors to where her pantheon of Hindu gods resided and spend
the rest of the day commiserating with them.

It was at this exact moment that I saw my neighbour Stan
Knowles running. To be clear, my neighbour Stan was not someone who ran. But here he was, huffing and sweating across the
parking lot. We watched him through the large glass window
facing Warden Avenue, giggling at his flop of hair, until I saw
his eyes and turned cold. He was running for me. I hoped I
was wrong, that he was there to see someone else, or he just
needed a Big Mac really, really bad, but when we locked eyes,
I knew something was horribly wrong and that it was Ba. I
didn't wait for him to get inside; I grabbed my bag and ran out
to meet him. I didn't think about how he had always creeped
me out with his jogging suits and sweatbands even though he
was, again, not in any way an active person. I tried to ask him
questions, but he was too out of breath. We sat in his car in
silence the whole way to the hospital.

As soon as I entered the private waiting room where Ma had
her head down praying with some of her *mah jong* friends,
I felt the empty space in the air. It was done. I didn't have to
ask. I just had to keep myself from floating away inside the
sudden weightlessness of the room.

The police came soon and told me some things. I nodded
and spoke to them. I was polite. I helped Ma sign their forms
and wished them a nice day. Then they walked away and I
left the waiting room. I didn't go anywhere in particular, just
followed the corners of each hall to the next, constructing my
own scene of the accident. I started with Ba leaving his office,
saying goodbye to everyone then walking toward the subway.
He would have passed the travel agency where the Disney
World brochures were lined up in the window. He would have
boarded his train, his old briefcase by his side and looked up

at the ads, probably searching for more Canadian things we could partake in. Then, when his stop arrived, he would have transferred onto his bus. The Scarborough landscape would have passed him by — the wide road, the shopping malls, the early summer weather. It was a gorgeous day, marked by gentle breezes and an impossibly blue sky. Maybe he hummed. Sometimes he did that. A familiar tune that made him feel sentimental. He loved The Platters. In my mind, I made him hum, "Smoke Gets in Your Eyes." He would have got off on his stop at Baymills and Birchmount, and, as he always did, instead of walking the extra hundred metres to the crosswalk, he jaywalked, just to get home those few minutes faster. As he waited on the curb, he probably thought about the word "jaywalk," probably playing with it as he liked to do with the origin of English words. Did the term "jaywalk" refer to a bird, perhaps a jay? Did jays take shortcuts? Maybe he felt like a bird caught in a stream of prey when he found himself crossing the street on his way home. Maybe he was a warrior, ducking and weaving between four lanes of cars, running and stopping. I imagined he loved how his body still knew how to twist and turn after a whole adult life of nine-to-five cubicle days. In the precarious state between life and death, in that moment, I thought he must have felt wholly free. This was my only explanation because no amount of scolding from Ma could ever stop him from taking that shortcut.

The moment he stepped off the curb, a baby blue '78 Firebird, emblazoned with red flames, threw him eight feet into the middle of the road. And there, two birds came head-to-fateful-head — a dodgy jay and a bonfire of feathers. Then all was still.

Some hours after all the papers were signed and the hospital staff had said their condolences, we went home. In the days that followed, I moved as if beneath water. Voices came in murmurs. People I knew and didn't know dropped by food that tasted like ground seashells, even soft Canadian noodle casseroles, even my favourite wok-fried vegetables. The light that seeped through the sheer curtains of the house threw everything into a ghostly grey-blue sheen. We were alone, together but separate, as we floated around the house.

There was a funeral, but it felt like I wasn't really there. It was more like a movie I was watching from a distance. I knew Ba's co-workers were there, the neighbours, Ma's church ladies. Everyone seemed so sad and could barely look at us, as though we were ghosts.

Afterward, Ma went to her room, attended to by a clutch of her *mah jong* church friends who all came out shaking their heads. No sounds emerged from this room, no crying, no talking, just a cold, jagged silence.

Without school, Sophia, Darwin, and I didn't know what to do with all the hours. Darwin played *Space Invaders* on his Atari while Sophia played staticky records on her record player. Sophia liked to play everything either too fast or too slow, which annoyed all of us. Her *Flashdance* single at 33 and 1/3 speed escaped under our bedroom door and seemed to moan quietly through the house. I re-read my stacks of *True Confessions* magazines, thumbing through the well-worn pages of cheating spouses, incest survivors, and middle-class kleptomaniac housewives. It calmed me to know there were screwed-up things happening in other houses with closed doors.

Sometimes, we found our friends tapping on the door, kicking at the ground. We knew they had come because their parents had made them. We would spend an hour in awkward conversation, maybe play some games on Darwin's Atari before they would leave. Soon, they stopped knocking.

Even Nida claimed she had so much to do to prepare for university in London, two hours away. I wanted to scream, "London isn't Siberia; you can buy deodorant when you get there!" but it wouldn't have done us any good. In my fake alternate universe, the one where Ba was not dead, I wondered if that other Miramar would be buying up deodorant and reams of paper as she prepared to go away to school too. I had been accepted at Carleton University in Ottawa. Now, I wasn't even sure if I would go.

After two weeks or so, the casseroles stopped coming, which was a relief because the freezer was full. Ma's friends only stopped in for quick visits in her bedroom. Silence fell a few degrees harder. On our own, the three of us kept the house clean and still ate our Lucky Charms cereal in the morning. We obeyed the eerie hush that had descended, tiptoeing around Ma and Ba's closed bedroom door. We raised our voices only occasionally to fight over the TV before the rush of events that brought us to that moment returned and muted us back.

Around this time, I felt the need to hold on to something of Ba's. One hot, humid day, I took his blue scarf from the hall closet and wrapped it several times around my neck to catch whatever of his warmth it still had in it and hold it there.

Darwin then donned Ba's fishing hat. It was beige with a tartan ribbon around it and was too big for Darwin's head, but he didn't seem to mind constantly pushing it off his face. Sophia chose Ba's green cardigan, the one that smelt like moth-balls, which we all associated with Hong Kong. She rolled up the sleeves three times and it hung on her like a bathrobe. We didn't talk about our new attire.

In the weeks after Ba's death, we used up the last of the cheques from Ma's wallet and I started to worry about the money situation. I scoured the closet and found a fresh book of cheques and Sophia forged Ma's signature so we could cash them. I assumed there must be enough in the account when the bank teller just shoved the money at me without blinking, but I had to wipe my sweaty palms on my jeans in order to take the cash. I found Ba's bank book and figured out how to pay the bills that were coming in and balance the account. Judging from my estimation, we only had a month's worth of money left. After that, I wasn't sure what we would do.

Chapter 4 ⚮

The eldest daughter has to shoulder the family. When all the men left to avenge their honour, Fan gathered wood and learned how to make fire.

AT NIGHT, WE SPOKE in whispers, and we talked about "it." Sophia and I shared a room, but when we found Darwin whimpering under the covers one night alone in his room, we dragged his mattress between our two beds. He had said he was just teary as a result of his allergies: "Ragweed season, ya know." I pulled him onto my lap like I used to when he was a baby and let him cry. I shooed Sophia away so he wouldn't be embarrassed.

One night, at about two a.m. when we all should've been sleeping, Darwin sat up and in a clear voice said, "I saw Ba."

The darkened room was illuminated by the plug-in nightlight. It cast shadows on my posters of Duran Duran and Sophia's numerous Madonnas.

"What d'ya mean, dummy?" Sophia hissed. She had a low tolerance for nonsense.

"I mean, Ba woke me up. He was standing right there," Darwin pointed to the foot of his mattress. "He said he just wanted to say hi, and to tell you guys not to worry because he's gonna take care of everything. He has big plans for us."

"Shut up. It was just a dream," Sophia still sounded annoyed, but her tone had softened.

"*You* shut up, stoopido. It was real. I even heard you and

Mir snoring, so I knew I was awake. He said not to wake you guys, that you wouldn't believe it. And he's right. You don't believe anything I say." Darwin sulked in the darkness. I heard the familiar clip of his nail against the side of his nose, and sure enough, even through the darkness, I could see him flick a piece of dried snot at Sophia.

"What else did he say, Dar?" I asked gently. I reached my hand down towards him and he took it.

"Nothing. He just said we were gonna be okay. Things are going to change, and that it's all part of the plan. Then he played *Super Mario Brothers* with me, and ate some of the tuna casserole that Mrs. Norway brought. He said it had too much Velveeta."

Sophia snorted, but I didn't.

"Do you think Ma's ever gonna come out?" Darwin said while gazing at Madonna. Darwin still needed Ma in those pragmatic childish ways. But I knew he would be okay. My worries were actually more for Sophia. She and Ma had always had a much more difficult relationship, locking horns over what Sophia wore, the friends she chose, and the music she listened to, but it was probably because they were so similar. When they were good, they were like the best kind of sisters. I remembered when Ma had taught Sophia how to sew, and how they'd spent so many afternoons bent over patterns spread over the kitchen table, their hair touching.

"Yah, Dar. I think she's gonna come out soon," I replied, without much conviction. Ma worked in extremes, which made her hard to predict. Sometimes, she was all organization and efficiency, whirling through cooking, shovelling the neighbours' walks, and hosting her *mah jong* group, and she'd keep all this up until she and her nerves crashed, like a wind-up doll that slowed down to a standstill. When that happened, she would stay in her room for days until Ba bundled her up in her robe and carried her to the car. They always did this late at night, after he was sure the neighbours were inside. He would return a couple of hours later or even the next morning, acting edgy, his usually neat hair looking like his fingers had raked through it over and over again. He would smell a bit sour, and his bloodshot eyes would droop.

We all learned the routine after going through it a dozen times. Ma would go away to a hospital — "Not a real hospital," Ba assured us. "A place to rest. That's all"— and come home after one week. She would return with dark circles under her eyes and thin as a grasshopper, but she would be better. Darwin, Sophia, and I would then hold our collective breath until she joined us in the world of the living. Until then, Ba tried everything to make life fun by cooking Hamburger Helper and letting us eat Twinkies. Darwin had been too young to be truly troubled by it, and I had been old enough to play along and pretend everything was normal, but Sophia scratched and scratched at her arms until they bled, and for a change, said little.

In another week, usually, Ma would be back at the *mah jong* table as if nothing had happened, making the Pope proud with her good deeds, and clipping the *National Enquirer* to show us the latest miracles. She had been especially impressed with the image of Jesus found on a piece of grilled toast in Texas. Ma had always loved her miracles. And Ba, for all their issues, truly loved Ma. It seemed that all he had ever wanted was to make her happy. Back in Hong Kong, Ba had liked to put a Beatles album on the turntable and dance around the living room, swooping us up to the lyrics, "*she loves you, yeah yeah yeah*," Ma's song. Eventually Ma would relax and shake her hips too. Clearly she'd been fun at some point before *Ka-La-Dai*; there was a photo in the album of her as a teenager wearing knee socks with the faces of Paul, Ringo, John, and George all over them. We kids used to fall into paroxysms of laughter whenever we looked at it. Now, thinking about it just made me feel sad.

With Ba gone, Ma was in charge. This thought made me feel

like I was falling from a tall building. Every so often, I would take a large gulp of air, realizing I hadn't breathed in a while. She might have been in charge, but she wasn't there, and this time, neither was Ba. I was the eldest, so as any book or movie would tell you, I was supposed to step up and take care of things. But I was supposed to be going off to university; that was my right. Now, I had a snotty brother and a snide sister and an absentee mother and a dead father and no idea what to do next. I resented that Ba hadn't visited me. He was probably still mad I hadn't backed him up on Disney World. Fuck Disney World, I wanted to yell. That's the *American* dream, Ba. This is Canada, which, by the way, is not all it's cracked up to be! I wanted to scream all this at him, to kick down doors, to let my hair loose and fly over the night sky, one leg outstretched as I arced over the houses, the mowed lawns, the stupid sedans, and across an empty moon. But instead I stayed quiet and very still.

Chapter 5 ~~

Bao was just a maid, a ghost of a girl who left clean floors and hot tea. No one saw her, but they were pleased there was always feast at the table.

TWO DAYS AFTER his reported sighting of Ba, Darwin ran out of the room while we were eating microwave pizza, picked up the violin from the corner of his bedroom and, with sauce still around his mouth, began to play. The torrent of stirring, striking music that flew with such fierce artistry from my brother's little hands was so lucid, so beautiful, it was almost horrifying. This, from a kid who normally rendered awful squeaks from the violin and hated his lessons.

We ran into the room, grabbing at napkins on the way. "What the hell was that?" yelled Sophia.

Darwin paused, his bow firm in the air above the strings, and with his wrist, pushed back the curtain of jet-black hair from his tiny face. We were all frozen. "That's not even your violin," squeaked Sophia. "It's the school's..." she paused. "But you normally suck at this." I could tell she was at a loss. She often spewed random facts when she didn't know what else to say.

"Darwin, where did you—" I started to ask before pausing at a shuffling in the hall. It was Ma. On one side of her head, the pillow had flattened her greasy hair so that it stood straight up. She was wearing Ba's pajamas and the extra length in the leg pooled on the floor. She looked sad and sweet, like a child, not nearly as bad as I had imagined she might.

Ma stood in the doorway and watched Darwin play, her eyes regaining focus. Sophia was still in the far corner of his bedroom, looking down at the instrument as he played. "So, what the hell was that?" Sophia repeated.

"Dunno," said Darwin shrugging. "I think I might have heard it on CBC or something." He went to put his violin back into its case when he looked up. "Ma!" he jumped.

Ma went to Darwin in fast steps. She held his face in her hands, looking down at him. Then, she hugged him to her body. I could tell that Darwin was uncomfortable by the way his eyes bugged out because Ma was squeezing him in an iron grip. "*Tsai tsai*," Ma said, "*Ho teng, ho teng.*" Little boy. Sounds good, sounds good. Then she looked disdainfully at the sauce on his face, released him and went to the kitchen to cook us a proper lunch. I was stunned on both accounts: first, by Darwin's freakish music, and then by Ma actually getting out of bed. Maybe things would be okay.

That evening, while Ma cleaned the house far more effectively than we had the whole time she was in bed, Darwin demanded to be taken to a piano.

"Dar, cool it, okay? Ma just came out. We'll find one tomorrow," I told him, nervously eyeing Ma as she plugged in the vacuum. She had even taken a shower and was looking almost like her old self, except that she was very thin.

"Mir, I've got to. Please, Mir! I need to…" Darwin implored, his hands flapping up and down as the vacuum started its loud *whir* that drowned out the rest of his voice.

He tried again, screaming this time, "Take me to a piano, damn it!"

The roar of the vacuum suddenly ceased. "What's that? What did you say, Darwin? Did you say a bad word?" Ma asked him, a hand cupped to her ear.

He ran to stand in front of her. "Ma, I need a piano. Right now. Please, Ma!" He bounced up and down, reminding me of when he was little and needed to pee.

Before he whined anymore, Ma had her apron untied. "Okay, okay Darwin, let's go."

Ma called a taxi and made the driver go super fast. Sophia, Darwin and Ma slid back and forth on the vinyl seat in the back while I gripped the handle bar in the front passenger seat for dear life and peeked every so often back at Ma.

"Hey, Ma, we don't have to go right now."

"No, no. Darwin needs a piano. Something is happening to him. We have to listen!" The cab made a sharp right turn into the driveway of the mall, the back of the car slamming and springing back from hitting the sloped pavement.

In the mall, we took Darwin directly to the music store. He walked along a row of pianos, running a hand softly over each one. At one black Yamaha upright, he sat down and his tiny fingers released a flurry of notes even as he struggled to reach the pedals with his feet. After he finished, we were once again stunned into speechlessness. A customer who had stopped in front of Darwin to stare, whispered reverentially, "That's Chopin's *Fantaisie-Impromptu.*" Sophia's mouth hung open. He got up from the piano and moved toward the percussion instruments. We followed him like zombies. He picked up random instruments and immediately launched into pieces of complicated music. Stringed, percussive, brass, wood — it didn't matter. He knew them all. Passersby in the mall, drawn in by the music, gathered around him in the store.

After Darwin let out an astounding rendition of Jimi Hendrix's "Purple Haze" on the electric guitar, the store manager ran to the phone and soon a CityTV news van pulled up to put Darwin on the six o'clock evening news.

Two days after the arrival of Darwin's miraculous talents, while we were eating our cereal, Sophia began to scratch out numbers and symbols on the Cheerios box with her scented markers. She stood from the table and within minutes had filled the leftover pages of her school notebook. Soon, strange scroll-like formulas that smelled like pineapples and mangoes began to appear on the walls, the floors, and even on the toilet seat. It didn't seem to alarm Ma at first, like it did me. She was too preoccupied with Darwin and his sudden talents. The phone had already started to ring with people asking if Darwin would make appearances at other music stores as a promotion. So I armed myself with spray cleaner and paper towels. The pens might have been meant for children, but their ink was permanent. Eventually, I would have to buy us another toilet seat, or start replacing Sophia's markers with pencils.

"What's wrong with you?" I asked my sister who looked possessed during these outbursts. Her one crossed eye was focused intently in a different direction than the other, making her look like a deranged Charles Manson. "Just stop that, already."

"I don't know," Sophia answered, before continuing her strange markings. "I can't stop."

In the middle of the night, I looked across at Sophia's bed and her fingers were moving, writing indecipherable symbols in the air. Even in sleep, she was becoming haunted by the strange formulas.

A few days later, she inserted her formulations, written on a long piece of construction paper, into a manila envelope and took her banana-seated pink bike to school. She wrote the name of her math teacher, Mr. Middleton, in block letters across the front and handed it to the school secretary. A week later, Ma got a call from Mr. Middleton, and could hardly make out what the man was trying to say because he ranted, raved, laughed, and wept rather than spoke. It seemed that Sophia had, by way of complex analysis, stumbled upon — "Oh no, quite the wrong word, Mrs. Woo ... hmm, discovered? Worked out? Yes, maybe worked out is more apt" — the most beautiful math theory there ever was: the Euler's Identity. Mr. Middleton had only heard of the formula from his days at McGill. He remembered his mentor, a Professor Gorky, lecture impassionedly on what he called the most poetic formula ever derived. The Euler Identity was sublime, a study of exquisite symmetry. It was, in short, perfect. Poor Mr. Middleton. He had been up all night since receiving Sophia's package, pulling down all his mathematic books from their dusty shelves. At the crack of dawn, he called Professor Gorky in Montreal and confirmed what he suspected. Sophia had gone about re-discovering it, even presenting new routes and possibilities in getting to it. He told all this to Ma, while Ma repeated all his sentences to us as soon as he said them.

"A fifteen-year-old girl!" he exclaimed over and over again. And I knew he wasn't simply shocked that it was from a fifteen-year old, but rather that it was brassy Sophia Woo who never finished her homework on time, smacked gum loudly even when she bold-face lied about having any in her mouth, and passed notes to her friends during his lessons. That was my sis. She always stuck one toe across the line of all rules, just to prove she could.

It was indeed, as he said, a miracle.

News of my siblings' sudden onset of "The Gifts," as we began calling them, spread like wildfire. After Darwin's TV appearance, other media outlets appeared at our door. Everyone wanted to get a piece of him, especially when they learned there were not one, but *two* child geniuses under one roof. These things didn't just happen every day in Scarberia. Our house was abuzz with journalists, Catholic priests, and experts of all kinds while curious strangers camped out on the lawn. Everyone had a theory about The Gifts. Among them was a woman completely dressed in white who claimed The Gifts were bestowed by an alien race that created humans as an experiment. She said Darwin and Sophia were the chosen ones to bridge the two species together. This prompted the priests to sprinkle holy water on everything.

The rush of people was both terrifying and thrilling. Ma insisted on making sandwiches for this mixed crowd, so I was assigned to slap Wonder Bread together with a lather of mayonnaise and a slice of deli ham. It goes without saying that Sophia and Darwin didn't have to help; no, they got to sit sweetly on the sofa and take questions while I served platter after platter of tiny square sandwiches. Ma insisted the crusts be cut, like they do in England apparently.

Sophia drank up the attention while Darwin kicked at the coffee table, occasionally asking Ma if he could be excused so he could play *Space Invaders*. The answer was always a hissed, "No," from Ma.

I decided to at least try and pretend my way into having a good time, so I assembled the sandwiches into mountainous heaps and humbly offered them to the guests, taking on a demure servant-girl shuffle.

The maid act, however, quickly became irritating. Soon, I was also taking orders for beverages, doing all the shopping for more supplies, making sure there was toilet paper in the bathroom, and being an all-around gopher.

Plus, the phone rang off the hook. Amidst sandwich-making and tea-pouring, I also took on the job of secretary, fielding the calls. Requests came flooding in from all corners of the globe. Professional child psychologists wanted to study Sophia and Darwin, academics wanted to apprentice them, and talk-show hosts just wanted to know everything. We even got a call from a producer at *The Oprah Winfrey Show*. I started to see the promise of all that offered money, buckets of it, enough that you could fill a room with banknotes and roll around for a few days.

"What do I do?" I asked Ma nervously. I didn't cope well with talking to authority figures, which, to me, felt like everyone. She told me to do what I thought was best for my brother and sister. Ma's job (according to Ma) was to sit beside Sophia and Darwin on the couch, a frozen grin on her face. In some ways, it was like she had been preparing for this kind of thing her whole life. There were two things Ma understood about the world as a Catholic: worldly suffering and miracles. Every time one of those commercials about starving children would come on TV, she would look satisfied as if she was infinitely wiser than everybody, and would turn to us and say, "See how lucky you are?" As for miracles, she had been waiting for them forever.

At night, when all the people faded from the house, Ma made declarations to us that she would be a servant to these extraordinary happenings. She would occasionally look to the heavens, her hands busily making the sign of the cross, and assigned these strange things to the holy Almighty. Even as she did this, I secretly wondered whether she also believed the craziness had something to do with Ba. She had a large photo of him set up on the coffee table and often smiled at him as if he were in the room.

When Ma realized that the media requests were coming in faster than I could respond to them, she rounded up her church friends and they fanned out like soldiers. They were delegated into different roles according to their skill sets: management, finances, media, and institutional liaisons. This new infrastructure worked like a well-oiled machine.

Chapter 6 ⌒

Shan's brothers were too gifted to stay in their little village when they could read and write. The emperor had called them to the imperial city to take up rank with his officials. She would never race, sweaty and happy, to the hills with them again. While she had expected that they would leave, she never considered what it meant to be left behind.

AFTER MA HAD ORGANIZED her battalion to manage The Gifts, there was nothing left for me to do. I waited, unsure of what I was waiting for.

"Ba is so proud," Ma told us, not seeming to notice how I was shifting uncomfortably from one foot to the other. I had done nothing new or special, but I guess she thought I could be a servant to the miracles, too.

No one said it, but it had been hanging in the air like a large question mark: what about Miramar? Wherever I went, to the mall, to the grocery store, or to the front of the house to water the lawn, everyone wanted to know about Sophia and Darwin. Mainly, people wanted to know what the early signs of genius were, and how to reproduce the conditions. Were they *normal* babies? Were they on a special diet? Did they get on well with others? How old were they when they began to talk? Read? Toilet train? Were there other people in the family with exceptional talents? Finally, they would ask if I had developed any extraordinary superpowers. No, I would reply, embarrassed, and take that as a cue to slip away.

The truth was, I was still waiting for my Gift. In secret, I tried to *will* something to happen. At night, I snuck out the window and laid on the flat roof of the house to face the stars, my arms stretched out, inviting the mysterious powers that landed on Sophia and Darwin to take me too. "Come to me. Come to me. Come to me," I beckoned the universe.

Once, I even tried to conjure Ba. None of us said it aloud, that he was probably responsible for all of this, but I think we all thought it, though we were scared to tread into such supernatural territory. "Ba, what about me?" I wondered. Silence echoed around me on the roof, and the stars seemed close enough to crush my chest. If Ba came to Darwin, it was clear, then, he didn't want to come to me. Perhaps it still had to do with Disney World, and Ba was holding a grudge, though I never would have thought he'd be so small about it. We were friends.

I reached my fingers out and touched the leaves of the maple tree we had planted when we first moved into the house. It had been a patriotic gesture, to commemorate our first home in the new country. The tree grew from a sapling to a full-fledged adolescent — awkward and graceful all at once. The top of the tree now hovered just above the roof of the bungalow. I held an unfurled young leaf in my hand then stuck a finger into the curl.

Beneath my disappointment of not receiving a Gift, I missed Ba. Why had he not given me something to hold onto? Something I could grow that would take the ache of his absence away?

And I was jealous. It ate through me like an army of green worms, occupying me like an invasion.

Once again, I faded into the background, something I was used to doing in the outside world, but never had to do within the world of the Woo. I was, at least, the eldest, which had some cachet, but I was also on equal footing with my siblings and

felt loved and was safe. Now I could barely look at Sophia
and Darwin because I thought I might scream or hit what I
imagined as smugness off their faces. My perceptions were
indulgent, I knew; Sophia was too self-absorbed to ever be
competitive with me. And I also knew Darwin was too sweet
to ever want to hurt me. Still, no one noticed me or the green
worms that had taken up residence in my heart. I continued
to serve sandwiches, and said nothing.

Scarborough was a decent-sized suburb, but it proved to be
too small to contain The Gifts. Several European and American conservatories wanted to meet Darwin and recruit him
into their schools. Professor Gorky wanted Sophia to start
right away at McGill in the Mathematics Department under
his tutelage while Yale and MIT also waged furious bids, up-
ping their offers of scholarship money. Ma and her friends
stayed up late into the night, playing *mah jong* and weighing
all these opportunities. As they clicked the tiles around the
table, debating the merits of each option, I sat on the stairs
eavesdropping in the dark.

Finally, it was decided. Darwin would take the Western European tour — London, Paris, Vienna, and Munich — but be
housed mainly at the Royal Conservatory of Music in London.
Sophia would go to McGill to Professor Gorky since he came
referred by Mr. Middleton.

Sophia spent hours deciding on which outfits to pack. Heaps
of clothes littered her bedroom floor. Her shoes alone wouldn't
fit in one suitcase — red Sparx high-top sneakers, the Nike
Wafers, ballet slipper flats, pink and yellow jellies, Cougar
boots, and all her sharp-toed pickle stabbers.

We had never been a sentimental bunch before, but a few
days before Darwin was scheduled to fly out to his new life,
he called us into his bedroom.

He sat down cross-legged on his bed and motioned grandly
that we should do the same on the other twin bed. I noticed

his old teddy bear that he hadn't played with in years sitting in his open suitcase. "No matter what happens, we have to meet on my birthday for the rest of our lives. No matter what. Deal?" he offered his pinky finger.

"Why your birthday?" Sophia asked with a scowl.

"'Cause it was my idea!" Darwin cried.

"How about this?" I offered. "We'll meet on Chinese New Year. Ba's favourite holiday. We'll do what we always did. Make pomelo lanterns, cook with Ma, fill the house with flowers.... That way, we'll be together every Chinese New Year for the rest of our lives. All of us."

Darwin seemed satisfied and lifted his little finger to lock on Sophia's.

"Swear," Darwin said to me. I crooked my finger through theirs.

"Swear," I replied.

"Swear," repeated Sophia.

"Hey, maybe we should do a blood oath, too," Darwin tilted his head to consider this.

"We're already related by blood, dummy," Sophia said, swatting him in the head.

Despite the gentility between us three siblings that night, the next day I bitterly added "bag carrier" to my list of servant duties, first accompanying Ma and Darwin to the airport in rush hour, and then, the next day, doing it again for Sophia at the train station. She wore a long scarf and sunglasses, looking every bit the movie star, and when I dropped her off and prepared to wave goodbye until she entered the building, she hefted her bag, turned and walked inside without a look back.

Now home alone for the first time in my life, I ate my cereal in front of the TV, left my things wherever I felt like, and every afternoon when I was finally ready to face the world, I went to the corner store and bought up every newspaper and magazine I could, clipping articles about my gifted siblings and pressing them into a scrapbook, waiting in my cocoon.

Labour Day came and went, and I was still wondering what I should do.

Chapter 7 ⁓

Ling wrapped her long hair tightly against her skull and donned her brother's hat. The only way to take the imperial exams and prove her worth as a scholar was to assume a disguise. She would laugh loudly and hork, spitting on the ground, and no one would ever know she was a girl.

IN MID-SEPTEMBER, I still wasn't sure whether I should go off to Ottawa or not. I had phoned Ma at her hotel in Helsinki to ask whether I should stay back in Scarborough with her, but she wouldn't hear of it. Or she could not hear it at all as our connection was really bad. But she did remind me that my going to university was what she and Ba had always wanted for me. Plus, she wouldn't be home for a while so what else was I going to do?

Over the crackly phone line, it sounded more like she was trying to get rid of me or just making sure I kept myself busy. When I had been accepted at Carleton two months before Ba died, they had treated it like it was the most momentous event of the year. We had gathered around the acceptance letter, Ma and Ba handling it like a sacred scroll.

Sophia and Darwin had also been excited about it for their own reasons. Sophia was thrilled to finally have her own room, and Darwin wanted to visit the Museum of Man in Ottawa to check out the dinosaurs. The ones in Toronto's Royal Ontario Museum, according to him, sucked eggs. All of us had been planning to spend a weekend at a hotel before launching me into my new life.

Going away to university was to be my thunder, my way of making some waves in the world. Now it was just a tiny drop of rain in a torrential downpour. Ma extended her trip to stay with Darwin through to Copenhagen where he would have a brief residency at some music conservatory there. In photos of Darwin in the newspapers, he held himself with a calm grace, looking perfectly humble and unaffected, like a Mozart in miniature. One review claimed that Darwin seemed otherworldly as the music that came from his tiny tuxedoed figure carried his audience to tears.

Sophia was now with Professor Gorky in Montreal where she was about to start at McGill on fellowship. She was about to become the star feature in the international mathematic forums for a season, and earn accolades from scientists and artists alike with her trademark sensibility for balance, her great cross-eyed beauty, and her penchant for off-the-shoulder sweatshirts. In the meantime, the matching luggage Ma and Ba had bought and had monogrammed with my initials on every golden buckle when I got accepted, sat in the hall closet still in its plastic wrapping.

I was going to have to lock the door, get myself to the bus terminal with all my quaint new suitcases, and pretend my family was still making the same fuss they had made all those months ago, all on my own.

After everything that had happened, I was hardly in any shape to start a new life. Between the grief snacking and the casseroles, I didn't have much to wear that still fit.

I surveyed myself in the mirror. My clothes were mainly made up of jeans and sweatshirts. Some of the zippers on the jeans were broken because I always bought them one size too small. The tighter, the better, I figured. Once, I tried putting them on in the shower so the denim would mould into my skin, but I had such an ordeal taking them off afterwards that I never did it again. Also, my legs stayed indigo for a week.

I folded the pants and put them into the largest suitcase. I could try all I wanted to achieve the long silhouette of the slender girls, but I would always look more like one of the seven dwarves. I did not have much of a waist, my hips flared way out and my bum ended near my mid-thigh in the back. Nida called me *womanly*. I hated that. I wished I had a body like Debbie Harry in Blondie: bone-skinny, all edges and points, like she hadn't eaten in a year.

I had wanted to get a new haircut before I left for Ottawa, but in the flurry of The Gifts I got derailed. My hair hung all over my shoulders like a forgotten lawn. My bangs reached the middle of my eyes, covering my glasses. I hadn't realized how often I was pushing strands off my face in order to see.

At least I still had my good skin. Ma often told me I should be proud of this feature. I sighed, looking at myself. I really didn't want to take this old Miramar to university, but like it or not, she was going.

I thought about taking the subway to the bus station, but I had more bags than hands, so I doled out some of my carefully squirrelled away money for a taxi and tried to keep my heartbeat steady.

On the bus, I sat back and watched the flat Ontario landscape roll by with its: endless fields and occasional cluster of cows. Sometimes, there would be a house, and a lone figure in the strands of grass. I wondered about the people who lived out there along the highway, and what it would be like to watch the world speed by yet remain so still. I felt lonely, more than I had ever felt before. I leaned my head against the cold glass of the window and thought of my friends.

My high school friends were all like me — a small cluster of Asian girls who also wore glasses, got As from the teachers who valued standardized testing (usually multiple-choice), and Bs among the teachers who wanted participation. We had collected each other along the way through junior high and high school. Instinctively, we had gathered, became friends, and bonded at the outer margins of the complicated social organization that was high school. We had eaten lunch together in the corner of the cafeteria, and talked about films and celebrities from Hong Kong, to Bolly/Hollywood. But mostly, we had talked about the small world of Holloway High — our classes, assignments, and teachers — while the rest of the school saw us as shadows pressed against the hallway walls, mere props to the larger drama of high school in which the popular kids were the stars.

Outside of school, though, we had been as randy as the next teenager. One of our favourite games was "Who'd you do." It always started innocently enough by Denise Pak — "Who'd you do? Mickey Mouse or Mighty Mouse? Fred Flintstone or Barney Rubble?" — but it would just as quickly devolve. Often times, it ended with Tina Chan refusing to choose between Mr. Troy (the Phys.-Ed teacher with B.O.) and Grant Banderby (the skinny nerd with acne who brought her gifts of his mother's homemade cookies wrapped in heart-shaped doilies).

We slandered the cheerleaders ("Sluts!"), the jocks ("Hunks of burning love but dumb as doorknobs!"), the brainiacs who ran student council ("Pretentious and annoying!"), and the beautiful people who didn't have to try very hard at anything but got first-rate everything ("Fated for tragedy sometime in their lives because they just had it too easy!"). We called ourselves the 4Somes, after a Hong Kong pop band by the same name, and also because there were four of us.

I could have used an afternoon with my friends just to gather their strength, but they had their own lives now: Nida was already at Western, Denise at Queen's University, and Tina at Centennial College. All we were to each other now was unfamiliar phone numbers on slips of paper floating around somewhere. And where was I? On a bus midway between home and Ottawa, a place I had never been and knew little about.

I pulled out the jam sandwich I had made myself and chewed

to my reflection in the window. Once in a while, the bus would pass a town with its rise of buildings, a few houses, a shopping centre off the highway, and then be back to fields again. Signs gave me my bearings. Places with old English names like Prince Edward County, Kingston, Cornwall, peppered with native ones, Gananoque, Petawawa, and finally, after five hours on the road, Ottawa.

The bus station was a closet compared to the station in Toronto. I spotted a single taxi parked across the street, so I dragged my three beautiful new powder blue suitcases across the pavement to get to it. The driver was chatty and in what seemed like mere minutes (was Ottawa really so small?), we pulled over to a mammoth red house set on a steep hill that resembled the house from *The Amityville Horror*. Looming on the edge of two-dozen uneven steps, the house looked like it was going to swoop down and eat me.

I couldn't help but imagine how things would have been if my family had been here. Ba would have gotten my luggage up the stairs in no time. Ma would have carried boxes of food, all neatly packaged in foil or freezer bags. And Sophia and Darwin would have agreed with me that I would definitely have nightmares in this place.

I took a deep breath. My suitcases thudded and scraped on every step.

Back when I had been accepted, I had lost the lottery for a dorm room, which meant I needed to find a place off campus. But with the commotion from The Gifts and Ba's death, I had forgotten all about dealing with that. When I had finally decided I would go to school after all, I realized I didn't have a place to live. I had agreed over the phone to this place the minute the landlord said, "It's still available."

I was going to be sharing the main floor apartment with three other people. When I opened the unlocked door, I was greeted by a petite woman in a printed tunic and leotards. She was perched on a chair on her tiptoes, wiping a hall window. I dragged in my luggage and shut the door.

"Well, hello, new roomie," she said, smiling. She hopped down, wiped her hand on her thigh and gave me the strongest handshake I had ever had.

"Um, hi," I stammered. "I'm Miramar Woo."

"Welcome, Miramar Woo! I'm Kathleen Longbridge. Obvious name for the kind of nose I have, eh? Well, I think it gives me dramatic flair," she turned to show me her profile.

Not knowing what to say, I looked down. She had on silver ballet slippers. Sophia would have immediately liked her. "Here, let me help you with these. I'll show you around." Kathleen grabbed hold of the biggest bag and gave me a pointing tour of the place while we walked to my room. It was hard to keep up with her because she walked as quickly as she talked. During the five-minute tour, I learned that she was an ex-cocaine addict, and had returned to school at the age of twenty-eight.

"I'm in English Lit. I'm a writer," she called over her shoulder while I followed. She had lived in the house for the last two years. The phone rang, and she dropped my bags in the doorway of what I presumed to be my room, turned around and skipped away. She waved at me, which I took as a sign that our conversation had ended. I dragged the rest of my bags into my new room and closed the door, exhausted.

Later, I met Lara, an architectural student with tattoos on her arms. "You'll never see me. I eat, sleep, and shit at school," she said.

I also met Dave, a freshman like me from somewhere called North Bay.

The house was settled into a hill, which made the apartment a semi-basement. I got the underground part, its only window a slit of light at the top of one wall. The room had a single mattress on the floor, a dresser, and a large wooden desk.

In the first two days, I stayed mostly in my room, sitting on the mattress and staring at the veneer-panelled walls. School wouldn't start until Monday, and I had missed most of frosh week. Unpacking took me three minutes. I thought about the posters of Duran Duran and Simple Minds rolled up in the corner and debated putting them up. In the end, I decided not to decorate because the emptiness of the room felt right somehow. All of life was reduced to this square. It was a good blank space from which to start again.

I could hear my housemates outside, chatting and laughing as if they'd known each other forever. Like normal people. I tried to make myself leave the room and join them, but frankly, they terrified me. What would I say? They were so different. Go out there and embark on this new adventure already, stupid, I told myself. Only when I worried they could hear my stomach growl through the walls would I finally emerge to cook dinner in the small kitchen. I cooked quickly, a pack of instant noodles from the giant stash Ma had insisted I take since I had never learned to cook. She had always said I would pay the consequences for not observing her more closely in the kitchen.

I made sure to clean my pot thoroughly before rushing back into my room to eat. I was afraid to use the phone to call Nida in case one of my housemates needed it, so I waited until late in the night to dial Nida's number in London. Nida, unlike me, was having a rocking time. When I got her on the line, our conversation was full of her animated stories of new friends, parties, frosh week, all told without punctuation so everything spilled out in one large rush. Afterwards, I tiptoed back to my room in the darkened apartment and pulled my covers over my head.

After a couple of nights, Kathleen knocked on my door. I peeked out while Kathleen tried to peek in. "Hey, whatcha doing in there? Come on out. Watch TV with us," Kathleen spoke as if she were talking to a wounded animal.

Not knowing what else to do, I said, "Okay," and followed her to the living room.

Dave was sprawled out across the couch with a can of Blue and scooted to one end when he saw me. He was large, over six feet, and looked odd as he tried to fold himself into a little package. "Hi, housemate," he waved.

"Hi." I gave a little smile and settled in beside him. *Magnum P.I.* was on the small TV that they had perched on a long wooden coffee table. The room was a motley collection of second-hand furniture, like the rest of the rooms in the house. Prints of the great masters hung on the walls. *Mona Lisa* smiled from one, and Monet's water lilies bloomed on another. I sat stiffly on the sixties-style green couch, my hands in my lap.

"Sooooooo," Kathleen began. "Who are you, Miramar Woo? Tell us about yourself."

I stared at the TV as Magnum, Tom Selleck, in his ubiquitous Hawaiian shirt, wielded a gun from behind a palm tree. "What do you want to know?"

That may have been too open-ended. I realized this instantly because it triggered a long list of questions from Kathleen who seemed to want to know a lot, while Dave just watched us with the dopey grin of someone who smiles when he doesn't know what else to do.

By the time Magnum had caught the bad guy and zoomed away in his Ferrari, Kathleen and Dave knew this about me: I was Chinese (I was accustomed to this always being something *gweilos* wanted to settle first). I was from Scarborough, a suburb of Toronto. I was eighteen years old. I had one brother and one sister. No, I did not drink, but it wasn't for religious reasons; I just hadn't ever been presented with the opportunity. Heroin? Nope, never. Not pot either. I liked to read. Novels, mostly. Sometimes magazines, but I didn't tell them about *True Confessions*. Yes, I liked to write (which made Kathleen very happy) and planned to major in Journalism.

Kathleen flipped her curtain of chestnut hair and sank her tiny frame into an armchair. She seemed temporarily satisfied. But then she sat up as if struck by lightning. "Wait. Your parents."

"What about them?" I asked.

"In what ways are they fucked up, and how did they fuck you up?" I would learn later that Kathleen minored in Psychology, which she drew on for her own recovery process. I swallowed, feeling a knot in my throat.

"My father is dead," I began. It was the first time I had said it out loud, and it felt wrong to hear it in my own voice. "He was killed by a car a couple of months ago."

The perma-grin dropped off Dave's face, and he took a long swig of his beer.

Kathleen just stared at me with unblinking eyes. "I'm so sorry, kitten," she finally said softly. No one had ever called me "kitten" before, but I could see in Kathleen's face that it was heartfelt.

"Same here, Miramar," Dave said. "That's rough."

"Thanks. It is," I answered. And just like that, the tears fell as if from an unclogged spigot. They fell in big sloppy drops on my arm and then onto the sofa where they made circles that bled into the fabric.

I felt Kathleen sit on the edge of the couch beside me, then her arms wrap around my shoulders. She whispered, "It's okay. It's okay, kitten," while Dave unfurled a roll of toilet paper, square by square, and handed the pieces to me.

Chapter 8 ⚬

She was called a good-time girl. If you were feeling weary, you could go to the teahouse and see Gin. She could put a smile on the most sour of faces with her songs, her quick jokes, and rice wine that she poured generously. What they did not know about was the thin blade of metal tucked into her sleeve. She was ready to roll with the good and the bad.

UNIVERSITY WAS LIKE entering a foreign country and I was the tourist. The campus was exactly what I had always thought a university campus would look like: green common spaces, a river bordering one side, a sprawl of buildings and a hive of students that set it alive. Ottawa in September was also exhilarating; the giant maples and elms dropped leaves the size of my hand, transforming the campus into a swirling vignette of gold, crimson, bronze, and corals. Sometimes, I had to stop walking just to experience being still inside such a kaleidoscope of colour.

My classes were enormous. We, the students, were shrouded in semi-darkness in the expansive lecture halls, pens hovering above our notepads, our eyes focused on the lit stage where the professors presided. Faculty was comprised of two camps: sixties hippies who had joined the establishment but were reluctant to admit they were comfortable, and old men who clearly had been there for a long time and took to the stage like royalty.

Most of my professors were of the former. My sociology

professor sat on a bar stool on stage, a mike in one hand and a cigarette in the other. He told stories for an hour twice a week, stories about being young in the sixties, listening to Allen Ginsberg first read his epic poem "Howl" in San Francisco's City Lights Bookstore back in the day; or, about being a draft dodger and how Canada was such a haven then for intellectualism and pacifism. "No more, no more," he lamented. Journalism 100 was taught by a fortyish woman who wore a long braid that trailed past her waist. She liked Batik-print dresses, and, under those, two hairy calves led to feet always encased in a pair of Birkenstocks. This professor used words like "verve," "erudite," and "caprice." She awakened something in me, and I later spent hours in the library researching the Beat Generation, feminism, South Africa, the Vietnam war. The more I read, the more I realized I had decades, contexts, and generations to catch up on.

In the first week of classes, groups of students set up tables in the large hall in the University Centre and advertised their causes. There were sororities and fraternities, all colour-coded depending on whatever Gamma Gamma Delta they represented. And then, there were the anarchists, the anti-apartheid activists, the gays, the lesbians, the Christians, the Jews, the "womyn." In yet another area, the international students' tables were draped with flags displaying their countries of origin.

I was curious. I envied the passion, the organization, the certainty with which these upper-year students held themselves. They knew who they were already. As a frosh, you were supposed to find yourself somewhere amongst these little tables, but I flitted quickly past, careful not to get too close or make eye contact so I wouldn't have to talk to anybody.

Kathleen took me under her wing and introduced me to her circle of friends. They were in their late twenties and had an air of "been there, done that" compared to the gangly first-years. They seemed infinitely wise. Kathleen liked to talk about her heady coke days. But she also confessed that her sinuses were a complete bust. "Burned holes right through my nasal passages," she proudly stated, tipping her face so I could look up her nose. It seemed so heroic when she put it like that. They took me across the river to bars in Quebec, where booze was cheaper and the clientele a tad sleazier. Fights were regular occurrences. The first time I witnessed one, I was in the line-up for the women's bathroom. Two biker chicks started brawling by the sinks, and they tumbled through the line and out onto the street. Kathleen and her friends continued dancing, laughing at my astonished face. "Com 'ere, kid," they said, and hugged me until my ribs hurt. Whenever I was with them, I felt like a favoured child in a commune.

Kathleen even gave me a mini-makeover. I conceded, even though it was understood that it wasn't because I was ugly; I just had the kind of looks that made me more background than foreground. Kathleen, luckily, was the grand dame of minor re-modelling. She took me to an optometrist and insisted I get a pair of contact lenses. Never mind that they cost me a whole month's budget for food. I did it anyway and ate crackers with peanut butter for breakfast, lunch, and dinner.

We left with my new contacts, and pushing my wayward hair out of my face, Kathleen said, "Oh, kitten. You look good. I mean, you were hot already, in a nerdy kinda way. But now! You look really good." She made a sizzle sound as she touched a finger to her bum. I somewhat understood what she was implying. Without my glasses, I didn't blend in as much with the other bookish Asians who went to Carleton.

Kathleen also taught me about makeup, telling me that lipstick was vital to the kind of day you wanted to have. There was a tube of Revlon's "Rosebud Rhapsody" in a desk drawer that Kathleen guarded with her life.

"Whenever I wear this, I swear I pick up someone, guaranteed. But I use it sparingly, so I don't overdo its magical powers."

She took me to the drugstore to find me my own special shade, and we settled for a pale pink called "Spring Blush."

When I surveyed my newly feathered hair (artfully curl-ironed), my naked eyes (but ringed in black), my skin-tight acid-washed jeans, and spring blushed mouth, I had to admit that improvements had been made. It was weird, and I couldn't say I was transformed into a head-turner like Sophia, but maybe, I thought, I wouldn't be furniture-grade invisible anymore.

In those first few months at school, there was so much going on, so much new attention from new people, so many fresh ideas rolling around my renovated head, that I sometimes forgot about my family or life in Scarborough entirely. Yet, at certain moments, something would catch at me. One day, I saw rabbits bounding through a field on campus. I had never seen wild rabbits before and hadn't even known they existed. We had had a bunny at home briefly as a family pet that Darwin named Gremlin. Gremlin had shit a maelstrom, so when someone stole her one day from the yard, we were actually all relieved. I remembered how Ba had told us that back home in Hong Kong people would eat bunnies. Ma had nodded and said, "No big deal. The Chinese eat everything. No waste."

After that, Sophia had spent weeks refusing to eat the meat on her plate even when Ba said, "Not us, Chinese," pointing to himself. "Those Chinese," he waved somewhere in the distance which we knew meant China. "Here, we eat Hamburger Helper!"

Silly moments like that, when they crept in for no real reason, would drill a dull ache into my chest, reminding me that the pain was still there. By being away from my family, I could almost believe that Ba wasn't dead, just somewhere else, but then something would snag the fabric of my day and everything would tumble back into clarity.

Sophia, Darwin, and Ma called occasionally, sounding happy. Even Ma who never wanted to go anywhere, seemed thrilled to be in Europe. She had taken a church friend, someone who spoke fluent English and had enough guts for adventure for the both of them. "Oh, Mir. *Ho laing*! So beautiful! Like postcards. The same!" she exclaimed across the wires. Meanwhile Darwin told me, "Mir! *Space Invaders* here is just like at home!"

Sophia was actually now living with Professor Gorky and his wife. Math prodigy or not, she was still young and they didn't like the idea of her having to live on her own, so they took her in. Since their kids were all grown, Sophia finally got her wish of being an only child. They lived in a massive brownstone in old Montreal where she got her own room with a giant bay window. They even had a cat named Big Joe who slept in bed with her.

"It's not easy being gifted, you know. There's homework — a crazy amount of it — and lectures and stuff. Plus, I'm not allowed to go the pubs because I'm *underaged*." She drawled out this last word as if that were the biggest injustice in the world.

These calls eased my mind and freed me to get on with my own life. For the first time, making friends was not the same angst-filled exchange at Halloway High where everyone checked each other's social status before embarking on a conversation. At university, we, the frosh, were little guppies sent to sea. Swimming against the current together, who was beautiful, who was smart, who was athletic, mattered less, or rather, it would take some time to sort out since there were just so many of us.

Liquor, I discovered, was also a great equalizer. After a few Long Island Iced Teas, I was elbow to elbow with geeks and supermodels alike. And damn it, I felt *interesting* when I was drunk. I liked the hazy glow that everything and everyone took on. I whipped my hair on the dance floor, smiled at everyone, and cracked jokes that made people laugh. That was a kind of power I had never experienced before. And I liked it.

Chapter 9

On his approach, his horse kicked up so much dust, she had to veil her eyes. When the dirt settled, Xue looked at him and saw a placid lake reflecting the moon.

THE FIRST SNOW came to Ottawa in late October, startling everybody into pulling out their mitts and scarves. It was around this time that I met Jerry. My housemate, Dave, often brought his friends home to watch hockey games. They were a lumber-jacket wearing, steel-toe boots kind of crowd, friends who all hailed from North Bay. I felt like I'd just stepped off the boat when I had to ask Dave where it was, since it was actually only four hours north of Scarborough. This place sounded like quintessential Canada, full of forests, lakes, rivers, canoes, and beavers. I suspected if Ba had known about it, we would have moved straight there.

Dave had one friend named Jerry whose soft brown eyes ringed with long dark lashes made him look like he was a sensitive sort of person. He wasn't the cutest of his friends, but there was a steady sweetness about him, like a boat you would trust to get you through a storm. Also, Jerry wasn't as loud as the other guys. He sipped his cans of beer like he was having tea with the Queen, and when he saw me, he always gave me a loopy smile. The first time we were alone, we shared a cigarette on the porch. I didn't smoke, but I was finding smokers cool, so I just held one and pretended, never inhaling.

It was a chilly night, and icicles hung thick to the edge of the house like a row of mismatched soldiers. The whole street was visible from our high perch at the front of the house on the hill. Smoke curled up from chimneys, and the smell of woodsmoke gave me the sensation that I was in some kind of Canadiana scene I had only known about from Christmas cards and Hudson Bay ads. All the elements were there: the cute boy in a striped toque, clear skies full of stars, our breath making clouds and mingling in the crisp air, the twinkling snow.

"So, like, what are you into? Music, I mean." Jerry squinted to keep the smoke from going into his eyes.

"I don't know. I like all kinds of things." I sensed that I shouldn't mention Duran Duran or Madonna. "What do you like?"

"I'm into the classics. Zeppelin, Rush, Crosby, Stills and Nash. That kind of thing. I play the guitar so, ya know, I'm into it," he said and took a long haul from his cigarette.

How to proceed?

"Um, so what courses are you taking?" I asked.

"Bunch of useless shit. Poli Sci, Economics, Law…all intro stuff. You?"

"Yeah, intro stuff…." Oh, God, I begged my courage, please do not fail me now with your lame shyness.

And then. Good lord in heaven, Jerry made it even better.

"Hey, wouldja look at the moon." He pointed his finger at the tall pine in front of the house. "See? It's so bright it's even casting shadows. Cool, eh?"

"Wow," I half-whispered in awe. There were long silver shadows laid across the sparkling white expanse of snow. This sent shivers down my back.

Jerry looked at me like he wanted to make sure I wasn't joking. When he realized I was sincere, a broad grin broke across his face. "Yah, nature's the best shit, eh?"

"Definitely," I answered.

Right then and there, I decided I was in love. And I decided I was going to try to get Jerry to love me back. In this new life, I was trying to believe anything was possible. I thought about it this way: if Darwin could be a musician, and Sophia could do math, hell, I could get a man.

In the days that followed, Kathleen was tipped off right away by the sight of my heavily painted lips. "Hey there, kitten. What's with all the 'Spring Blush'? You crushing on someone?"

I confessed, thinking Kathleen would be a worthy mentor in my project to get Jerry.

"Play it cool, kitten. Guys love that. Don't just give it away," Kathleen said sagely.

Dave had no clue. He just thought I was taking a sudden interest in hockey, and really, from his perspective, why not? I learned quickly about hat tricks, icing, and power plays. I learned to recognize when a penalty was the right call, or if the ref was just being an asshole. These things mattered, I began to realize, and made a mental note to add them to the list of things *gweilos* liked. But aside from the occasional cigarette between periods, I rarely got time alone with Jerry.

One morning over toast, Kathleen decided we should have a party. "Here's your chance, kitten," she winked.

Kathleen and I were going to prepare all the food. We would have a proper sit-down dinner for twenty with candles, a nice table cloth, everything. Afterwards, we would play music, dance, drink, and stay up until dawn.

"It's going to be bloody perfect," Kathleen pronounced.

We made a lasagna the size of a small car and a three-tiered chocolate cake. Others brought salad, chips, beer, vodka, and drugs. Apparently, there was a dry spell on weed, but hash was plentiful.

That night, everyone was in a great mood. The North Bay boys inhaled the food like they hadn't eaten in a year. The laughter washed over me like a warm bath. This is what it was like, I thought, "it" being the catchphrase of my new life. "It" meant being an adult, having friends, putting on a dinner party. "It" meant this delicious heat that was warming me from the inside out. I looked around and everybody seemed so beautiful in the flickering candlelight. I was smiling so hard that my face hurt from pure happiness, until Jerry, who had been strategically positioned next to me, nudged me and told me I was cute.

"You're cute too," I murmured back. We stared at each other. It was all coming together.

After dinner, everyone fanned out to all parts of the house. Some people started dancing to Van Halen in the living room, others sat on the floor in little groups. Some were in the kitchen heating knives over the stove and dropping hash on them and then inhaling the smoke. Jerry and I continued to sit at the dining-room table and talked about how cool the band The Tragically Hip was. Suddenly, he kissed me. I was startled by the softness of his lips; it was like kissing a marshmallow. I pulled back and looked at those lips, now covered in the "Spring Blush" I'd been assiduously reapplying throughout the night, and began to laugh.

Jerry said, "You're a really goofy girl." I didn't know what to say, only that my face felt completely contorted from smiling so wide.

"Yah, definitely goofy."

We kissed again which lead to a full on make-out session until someone yelled, "Get a room." We stayed where we were, our mouths mushed against each other. My back started to cramp from being swiveled in my chair, but I didn't care.

Later, we resurfaced and found most of the others had slipped away. Emboldened by vodka tonics, I grabbed Jerry by the hand and took him to my room where we fell on the bed and rolled around with our clothes on for what seemed like hours, or at least until my lips were chapped and my buzz had worn off.

Finally, Jerry said, "Hey, I've never been with a Chinese girl before. Have youse ever been with a white guy?"

Hell, I thought, I've never been with anybody — white, Chinese, human. I had only ever practiced kissing my stuffed bear, Momo. I wished he had never said it. I was temporarily knocked off my nice ride. "Um, no," I told him.

He seemed satisfied with that and started to kiss my neck. Okay, now I was back on track. I was feeling a lovely ache between my legs.

"I've got something, if youse want to do it," Jerry murmured from my neck. Got something? Do it? Like, really do it? I thought about it for less than a second. I had wanted to lose my virginity since I was fourteen. I may have appeared as mild-mannered Miramar Woo, slightly overweight, silent girl in the halls of Halloway High, but at night, in the privacy of my bed, with Sophia snoring and Momo by my side, my fingers between my legs, I was a fervid vixen of the nth degree. Do it? Hell, yes!

Two things I had not expected: how mechanical the motions of sex were, like a water pump, and how prickly sweaty skin on sweaty skin felt. Then there were more things I didn't expect. Like, why did sex not feel as good with someone I liked as it did by myself? That was the biggest mystery. There was no pain, no blood, none of the fanfare that I had read about in *True Confessions* or seen in movies. I wasn't swept into a tidal wave of love and dreamy surrender. Just a blunt soreness. While his fingers travelling my body like a car without a road map were delicious, on the whole, the event was, unfortunately, anticlimactic.

"Was it good for youse?" Jerry asked after rolling off me and peeling off the condom. I looked at his back, freckled like cinnamon had been spilled on him.

"It was good," I replied.

"Cool," he smiled, relieved, before searching for his jeans on the floor, and plucking his smokes from the front pocket.

It seemed all right that I lied. It even seemed all right that the much-anticipated fireworks didn't explode in my body in my first ever attempt at sex. It was more than enough that once it was over, I had this man lying next to me, his leg looped over mine as we passed a cigarette back and forth.

Chapter 10 ⤚

When love finally arrived, Lu could not stop touching herself. Brushing her fingers across her cheek, she would smile at the memory of her lover's embrace. She could summon a summer storm across her body just by thinking of his arms.

AFTER I SLEPT with Jerry, I was wracked with anxiety as to how to keep him and make him mine. I started to spend more time assembling my wardrobe than hitting the books. This made no sense since Jerry always looked the same. He had two pairs of identical Levis and two shirts: one red plaid and one brown plaid. Sometimes he wore a blue sweater that he pulled over whatever plaid shirt he was wearing and always the same baseball cap that said "Furrow Flames," his high-school team. By team, I assumed he meant hockey because that was all the North Bay boys ever seemed to talk about.

I didn't care what clothes Jerry wore. To me, he was perfection. I found myself staring at him when we were together. His long, tapered fingers. The web of lines at the corner of his eyes. His pink lips.

"What are you doing? Youse making me nervous, girl," he would blush. I got embarrassed when he caught me, but I couldn't help it. He looked so god-awful beautiful to me that I felt my heart cracking when I took him all in. I started imagining what our children would look like.

When we weren't together, I felt jittery, like a junkie without a fix. Or, at least, that was what Kathleen said. I couldn't study, I couldn't sit still, I couldn't think. I was only truly alive when he and I were together.

"Be careful, Mir," Kathleen warned. "He's only one guy in a sea of many. Don't get too wrapped up."

"What are you talking about? I'm in love," I argued. Wasn't this the way people in love behaved? She was usually so carefree; why was she being such an asshole? She was the one who had helped me get Jerry in the first place.

"Okay, do it your way," she sighed as if I were a delinquent teenager. I fumed. Who was she to tell me how to do anything? For all her expertise in trapping men like butterflies in her careful net, Kathleen didn't even have a steady boyfriend, just a stream of lovers that flitted in and out of her life.

Kathleen wasn't the only asshole. I told Nida everything about Jerry, but she didn't have much to say, and what she did say was all wrong. "Where the hell is North Bay anyway?" she asked.

"Why do you say it like that? North Bay's a place. In Ontario. Hello? Do you have to be such a Toronto snob? Besides, we're from Scarborough, hardly an exotic place on the map."

"Okay, okay, whatever. I was just asking…" she trailed off. "So, anyway, how are your classes? Didn't you just have midterms? How'd you do?"

Truth was, I didn't want to talk about school because I was royally messing up. My grades were dropping at an alarming speed. "It's fine," I lied to Nida who was trying to keep her own GPA high enough for an MBA program.

"Okay, well, have fun with Jerry. I have to go. Got a study group in ten minutes. Talk to you soon."

I could not figure out why everybody was being so stupid, especially when I was finally happy. Like, really, really happy. They were jealous, I reasoned. There was no other explanation. I decided to take the high road and forgive them since they obviously didn't have anything close to what I was experiencing.

Still, there was the matter of my grades, which I was actually getting a bit worried about. Jerry was certainly no scholar. He had failed three out of five classes in the first term. The second term was barely underway and it didn't look promising. Jerry was not stupid; he just wasn't particularly interested in school. "I'm just not a bookworm like youse, Mir," he complained. There was something about the way he said this that made me feel as small as I had felt back in high school.

"No, it's just that you're not trying. Let's go to the library and look up some of these books," I urged. I had always been my most comfortable between the stacks. For a while, I was determined to make him love the feeling of cracking the spine of a book as much as I did. I started doing all his essays along with my own. I kept asking him to try harder. He would just pop open another can of beer and smirk. So I did the barest minimum of work, cramming all my studying and essay writing into all-nighters before assignments were due so I could spend time with Jerry instead. Still, Jerry thought I was an overachiever.

I was noticing that Jerry didn't just dislike his classes; he was pretty well indifferent to everything about university or Ottawa as well, preferring to hang out with his friends from "back home." Most of Jerry's stories began with the words, "Back home." If North Bay seemed like a foreign country to me, then Scarborough would have been another continent to Jerry.

One night, we went skating along the canal that snaked its way all through the city. The lights cast warm yellow pools on the ice, and the air crackled from the cold. Fog rolled along the surface, making everything appear fairy-like. I held onto Jerry's mitted hand as we glided towards the twinkling lights of downtown.

"Ya know what I really miss?" Jerry asked before answering his own question. "The bush. I seriously miss the bush."

I thought about this for a few seconds. "Which bush?"

"North Bay," he replied.

"Yeah, but which bush in North Bay?"

Jerry stopped skating and looked at me like I was high.

"North Bay's bush," he said.

"But isn't there more than one bush? Wouldn't a place like that have lots of bushes?" I was beginning to wonder what the hell we were talking about. Then Jerry started laughing. He laughed so long and hard that his skates gave out from under him and he went tumbling down, dragging me with him.

"Geez, girl. The bush means *the woods*. Ya know? Where we hang out, go camping. *The bush*." Jerry was still laughing.

"Oh, the bush," I repeated, forcing a laugh. I didn't think it was funny. Why would you call the woods "the bush"? The bush simply conjured up images for me of the neat hedges our Scarborough neighbours kept trimmed.

I would have felt truly stupid if he hadn't picked me up, dusted me off, and wrapped his arms around me from behind so we skated as one. We were from two different worlds; we should not have found one another or come together the way we did. But I believed, as we held tight to each others' bodies and glided over the bumpy ice, that we were beating our own odds.

My deepened sense of romance about us was furthered every time we had sex. It just got better and better the better I got at it. I couldn't get enough of Jerry's body on mine. I needed him to be with me. Needed him with his tongue thrust in my mouth and his hips tucked between my legs. I inhaled him deep into me. Only Jerry could have stopped me from getting more.

"Aren't you tired, girl? Shit. You are some kind of sex machine or something." He would shake his head while I licked his chest. I would devour him if he would let me.

I was convinced that this desire was changing me. Kathleen remarked on how bright my eyes were, like two beams of light shooting out of my head. I believed her. I felt like a feral animal, perpetually hungry. When we were not having sex, I was just waiting for the next time we would. I didn't mind that once we were done, Jerry would pick himself up, get dressed, and go out to where his friends were watching TV or drinking beer. I believed he was putting up appearances, but, in bed, with me, was where he was most at home.

Because the North Bay crew was so often around, it was as if I was dating the whole crowd of them. To spend time with Jerry, my life became his routine. *Hockey Night in Canada* at least twice a week, and then to a series of pubs they frequented to pass the time away. His friends were nice enough, but I didn't always understand their conversations: people they knew in their hometowns, drinking games that they thought were funny, and sports mishaps from seasons gone by. What mattered the most was that I was with Jerry. Whoever happened to be there was just backdrop.

I studied other girlfriends to see if I was doing it right. There was a way they looked at their boyfriends — an upward tilt of the head, a coy smile, a playing with the eyes, a giggle that I could never fully master. A touch on the arm meant, "remember you're with me." A touch on the leg said, "I want to be alone." Clever one-liners were heavy with sexual innuendo. There were a million fine details that went along with being someone's girl. While some maneuvers I was better at (the shy looking up, a Princess Diana move), other endeavours were less successful (my giggle sounded like a hyena's).

So I took care of Jerry. I cooked him macaroni and cheese. I went to his classes with him and helped him take notes and wrote his essays. I cleaned his two plaid shirts. Once, I overheard one of his friends say, "You have your own personal geisha girl, Jer." They all laughed, thinking I couldn't hear because I was in the kitchen fetching Jerry a beer. I heard fine, but I didn't care. As long as Jerry wanted me, everything was wonderful.

Jerry lived on campus, where he shared a room with another student from up north. But when he got too drunk to find his way back home, I would guide him lovingly to my place. On one beer-soaked night, Jerry disclosed to me that his father beat him. Not just when he was a kid, but even now, as an adult. And not just a wallop to the bum every so often, but episodes that involved whipping a belt against his back, crashing furniture over his head, and holding a broken bottle against his throat. Jerry's dad was a drunk, a good-for-nothing wife-beater. His mother had long ago split, and had left Jerry and his little brother to their own survival devices. Jerry had done everything possible to get the marks to get into university. And the night he told me all of this, he sobbed into my lap, snot and tears soaking my acid-washed jeans. I stroked his hair and vowed silently that I would love him even more.

After this, I finally began to open up with my own little stories about Scarborough. Like how it had been when we first bought our house and my family would sit on the curb, eating from a bucket of Kentucky Fried Chicken and gazing at the frame of our house as it was being built. We had imagined what each room would look like. Sophia and I had decided to paint ours pink, of course. Ma had wanted to plant a garden in the small backyard to grow tomatoes, beans, and roses. When we finally moved in, it was spring, and one day, men came in trucks and rolled out dozens of grass strips on the dirt. Sophia had marvelled at this and thought grass was carpet for the longest time.

I also tentatively told Jerry about Ma's nerves, and how one day, shortly after we had moved into the house in Scarborough, Ma began to hallucinate. The first episode had come after an incident at the Woolco cafeteria when I was ten. It was $1.44 day and we had been on a back-to-school shopping mission. After selecting new socks, underwear, sweaters, and the infinitely important Laurentian pencil crayons in the requisite twenty-four colours, we had stood in line at the lunch counter as a special treat. I had been entranced with the rice pudding, a congealed paste of yellowing white in a glass dessert dish, topped with three wiggling raisins and covered in Saran Wrap. Darwin had been all about the french fries, and Sophia had chosen the hot chicken sandwich drowned in brown gravy, all highly coveted foods we never got to eat at home. We had slid our trays along the stainless steel counter and ordered from the ladies in hairnets.

After Sophia got her stringy chicken, sandwiched by white bread with a pile of brown steaming goop on top, we heard the shouts from one of the tables. "Go back to where you came from," the kids had sniggered.

We had snapped to attention, our backs like steel rods.

Ma had whispered to us in Cantonese, "Don't look. Just ignore."

But we couldn't help it. We had to look. I snuck a peek while Sophia turned fully around to face them. There they sat, three white boys, maybe sixteen or seventeen years old, nursing milk-shakes and blowing the pink and brown goop at each other with straws. They had laughed and pointed at Sophia. My face had flushed with heat and I had begun to shake. Darwin had looked up at Ma. Then Sophia, with all the might in her seven-year-old body, had shouted back at them, "Shut up, you bloody asshole. Bloody, bloody, hell assholes," she screamed. It was every curse word she had ever learned in her young life, thrown together like a salad.

Not a second had gone by when Ma reached up and slapped Sophia across the face with such force that she wavered before falling, dragging her lunch down with her to the ground. She sat on the floor, clawing at the gravy burning her face and arms, chicken pieces and soggy bread all over her clothes. The teenagers had collapsed into heaving laughter that reached into my body and made me feel sick.

Sophia had then stood up, letting the food fall from her, and in a low voice that was cold and steady, she turned to Ma and said, "I hate you."

I had kept my eyes straight ahead, looking past the counter to the server's face. The server had a scoop of mashed potatoes in her hand, a plate in the other. She froze the moment Ma had slapped Sophia. The old woman's eyes had filled with horror. I had wanted to shout, "This is all wrong! It's the boys, the boys are to blame!"

The cashier had rushed over with a wet cloth and proceeded to clean up Sophia, clucking quiety, "Tsk, tsk. You poor dear." Another staff person appeared, and the teenagers were asked to leave. I had heard about things like this happening, but my eyes remained locked on the server's face. Finally, the server turned her eyes on me and startled, as if she had seen a ghost. I was not sure what my face looked like in that moment, but I guessed it must have been horrible.

That night, Ma met what came to be known as "the hands." At first, she told Ba that a pair of hands was following her. The pair became a hundred, then a thousand, then countless, all lurking in the shadows. They would make obscene gestures, slap at her, and pull her hair. Ma had become terrified, staying in bed with the blankets pulled over her head to escape them. She kept asking to go home, over and over, getting louder and more frightened. We heard her through the bedroom door.

Later, Ba had asked us what had happened at the mall that day, but we just shrugged our shoulders and avoided each other's eyes. We were too scared and confused to know what to tell him. Maybe it had even been our fault.

After that, no one could predict when the shadows would strike. It was random. Things could be okay for months and months, to a point where no one even worried about it any-more, and then, furtively, like animals coming out to prey at night, the hands would return. I told Jerry that this was what had troubled me most since Ba died. No one knew when the hands would come back to claim Ma. I didn't know how to handle it. I didn't want to have to. I wanted Ba to do it.

I had never told this to anyone, but I told Jerry. There was a part of me that knew it would be impossible for him to understand, but I wanted him to, so badly.

"Aw, baby. People are just shit, ya know." He shook his head with his arms around me. "There're just some shitty, shitty people in the world."

I nodded. Jerry was sweet, but I knew he really didn't get what happened in Woolco or my family.

I didn't think any outsider could understand if he didn't know my family, but it was not like I could sit and chat with Ba about our stories. But I realized I needed to tell the stories, even just to remind myself of who I was.

Chapter 11 ⚊

They did not recognize her as a princess. For her own protection from the Emperor's enemies who wanted to overthrow him, Qian had to don the clothes of a pauper and walk among the common people. Her mother, the Empress, would not allow her to fight with her father's army, thinking her only child needed to live to continue the royal lineage. To the villagers, she was just the lowly daughter of the pig farmer, smeared in dirt and manure. She longed for her blow-dryer. She longed for her Chanel N°5. Instead, she shovelled pig shit and tolerated her own stench.

ONE JANUARY NIGHT of that first school year, in the middle of *Hockey Night in Canada*, a commercial previewed an upcoming feature news story on CBC: "Two geniuses. One family. An Immigrant Success Story!" Then came a shot of Darwin in his little tuxedo as he stood with a violin on a lit stage, a full orchestra behind him. The next shot was of Sophia standing on a chair in front of a large blackboard in a lecture hall, scribbling a series of symbols and numbers while a hundred people in the audience sat on the edge of their seats, riveted. "Watch CBC news at eleven." Still too absorbed in the hockey game, the North Bay boys didn't even notice the commercial.

I spent the rest of third period in a sweat, debating whether I should tell them or not. The New York Rangers and the Toronto Maple Leafs bashed it out on the ice while I bashed it out in my head. On the one hand, I was really proud of Sophia and Darwin. On the other hand, I would have to explain The Gifts, and they would probably wonder why I wasn't special. For the first time in my life, I had been feeling like I actually was special. I was special just for fitting in so seamlessly in this new world. I didn't want to tip the balance.

The Rangers won. The boys sat dejected, and their Leafs jerseys looked just as deflated as the boys slumped over their beers. The predictable post-game chatter came on, but with a 7-0 loss, there really wasn't much to talk about. When first the commercials, then the familiar CBC signal came on, the North Bay boys started moving around, getting restless for the next activity. Watching the news wasn't usually on the agenda after games. But then. The story began:

"One family. Two child prodigies. Less than a year ago, life changed forever for the Woo children when they discovered their extraordinary talents, which took them from Scarborough, Ontario, to the concert and lecture halls of the world."

First came a shot of Darwin with the violin under his chin. His vigorous playing of Vivaldi's *The Four Seasons* rocked his small body back and forth. He had gotten new glasses, I noticed. They were round tortoiseshell frames and made him look like a child playing grown-up.

"Holy shit. Look at that kid." Dave pointed at the screen.

Then came a close-up of Darwin's round face. His hair was still too heavy for him, like a black lid on his head, and he smiled widely for the camera. He was wearing the tuxedo, the one that a tailor had custom-made for him for his first concert performance. The interviewer asked him what music meant to him. Dar shrugged and said in his high voice, "It's a living." The North Bay boys howled with laughter. When asked if there was anything else he wanted to say, he waved frantically at the camera and yelled, "Hi, Miramar!" Then the North Bays boys stopped laughing and stared at me.

Next was a shot of Sophia lecturing a group of undergrads. She was wearing one of her signature off-the-shoulder sweatshirts. Sophia was always proud of her ability to cut up these sweatshirts so they hung just right. It looked like she had gotten a perm and her luxurious hair now hung in ringlets all over. "Hey, is that chick cross-eyed?" one of the boys laughed. "Shut up," Jerry snapped.

Then came the narrator again: "Sophia Woo, at the tender age of fifteen, is a part-time lecturer at McGill University. She completed her doctorate in a mere four months, astounding the mathematical world with her genius."

"Tell us, Sophia, when did you first realize you were a genius?" the interviewer asked. They were sitting in an office, Sophia's office, I assumed. Behind her stood a large blackboard covered in different coloured chalk markings — Sophia's formulas.

"Since as early as I can remember I knew I was special. I just didn't know in what way until the math hit me," Sophia smiled demurely. She looked beautiful.

"Hit you? Is that how you would best describe it?"

"Sure, it wasn't there one day, and then suddenly it just happened. Numbers and symbols started floating around right here." She touched her forehead. "They had to come out. It was like a *Tetris* game, ya know? All the numbers had a place and they just *fit*."

The narrator talked a bit about Scarborough and flashed scenes of strip malls and of our old high school. "From this suburban neighbourhood came the wondrous talents of these two extraordinary children." The scene switched to Ma. "What do you think of your kids?" Ma stood on a stage in front of a piano. Darwin sat next to her on the bench.

"My children … they work hard," Ma said. "I am proud." This made my eyes well. And me, Ma? I wondered. Are you proud of me, too?

"Do you worry about them? I mean, peaking so young?"

"Peking? No, no, we from Hong Kong. Not Peking," Ma smiled, shaking her head. I knew exactly what my mother was thinking: *Gweilos* think we're all from Beijing.

The narrator concluded: "There you have it. An immigrant success. A wholly Canadian story."

The scene closed with another shot of Darwin playing the piano on the same stage. This time the narrator said it was Joseph Haydn.

"Whoa! Miramar! Was that your family?" Dave asked. Kathleen was sitting on the edge of her seat, her eyes wide. Uh-oh, I thought. More psychoanalyzing was going to come out of this.

"Yep," I shrugged, trying to look casual. They all started talking at once.

"Wait. One at a time. I can't hear all of you." I held my hands in front of my face.

I thought I would have to field questions, but they mainly had comments. The general consensus was that it was "really cool."

"Now I get why you're so smart. It's in the genes," Kathleen said warmly. They all agreed, calling me a brainer. I laughed with them. I couldn't believe that they thought I was special enough just as I was. I didn't elaborate on the circumstance of The Gifts. I didn't know how to explain that, and I sensed the CBC producer didn't either since Ba had not come up.

Jerry swung his arm around me. This should have relaxed me, but instead, a panic grew. They were just being nice, I thought, and were really wondering what was wrong with me. The North Bay boys told me they thought Sophia was really hot, and that Darwin was a real hoot. They even said Ma spoke excellent English. I stuffed down my insecurities. I should have just been proud of my family. I should have just said, "Thank you." There were a million "shoulds" in the world, or in my world anyway, but they didn't add up to squat. I was still the same boring Miramar Woo from Scarborough. Some things were no different.

Chapter 12 〜

Wen was drunk with love. She absent-mindedly mopped the floors, leaving streaks of dirty water across the stones. She burned the rice and received a slap across the face from the mistress. Her eyes were fevered, and her head was hollowed. She paid no attention to anything else but the thought of how to keep her lover from leaving her. Her friend Pat's words reverberated – love really was a battlefield.

ALL THAT WINTER, Kathleen took to knitting. On some nights, when Jerry didn't call, I would sit with her in the living room while she taught me. We made long scarves that fell down our laps, snaked across our legs, and swam all over the floor around us. Kathleen said she hated to finish the scarves because they were just so pretty. She chose her colours and yarns carefully — lilacs matched with purples and blues and greens. Mine were all solid colours since I didn't yet know how to change yarn. The one I was working on was already too long, but I decided I would not finish it until I heard from Jerry. It had been a full three days.

Kathleen took these opportunities to talk about her ex-boy-friend whom she referred to as "The Love of My Life," "The Only Man I Really Loved," or "William Dexter Michael Rowan."

"We were meant for each other, you know. The moment I laid eyes on William Dexter Michael Rowan, I knew he was my soulmate. You know about that, right?" She looked over at me for confirmation. I nodded, but didn't take my eyes off my needles.

"When we are born, our souls are divided into two pieces. Your other half is floating around in someone else and it's our life's mission to find them."

I stayed silent. Where the hell was Jerry? He was supposed to call at seven p.m. and it was now seven-fifteen.

"So I guess I was lucky that I found The Love of My Life so young." She smiled into her needles. "God, there was just recognition, ya know? Like, we were just two people adrift, wandering aimlessly and then, BAM! There he was at the Red Clover Pub one night when I least expected it...."

Seven-seventeen p.m.

"It was more than sexual attraction with us. I mean, don't get me wrong, the sex was great, but it was so much deeper. Like, we were so spiritually connected. I knew what he was thinking before he even thought it. Sometimes, we didn't even need to speak. We just lay there and looked into each other's eyes...."

Seven-twenty-one p.m.

"Meeting The Only Man I Will Ever Truly Love was and will always be the biggest thing that ever happened to me. I will never love like that again. No one will ever come close to a love that big. And now that we're apart, my soul has been torn in two again."

Seven-twenty-four p.m.

"So, what happened to him, Kathleen?" I asked her just to keep myself distracted from looking at the clock again.

"Huh?" She looked up at me.

"What happened?"

She looked down and caught her stitch and continued to knit. *Click click click.* "Well, we were just too into coke. After I had a close call, my parents kidnapped me and sent me to detox. William Dexter Michael Rowan started banging Shirley Jameson while I was away."

Click, click, click.

"He was just too out of it, see? He really loved me, but he was messed up. I mean, The Love of My Life was living on the streets. Last I heard, his brother got him out of Ottawa and took him to Texas. His family wouldn't let me contact him. Said we were toxic together. Whatever. They don't get it."

Click, click, click.

"Anyway, there's a reason I am telling you all this, Miramar. Don't get so sucked up by love. Look at me. I am a broken soul." I looked at her radiant skin, her abundant chestnut hair, her teeny perfect body. I thought about the effect she had on the men who swarmed to her and wondered what the hell she knew about being broken.

"So, what you're saying is that Jerry and I are toxic for each other?"

"Not necessarily. I mean, take your time. If I knew what I know now, I would have said to The Only Man I Really Loved, 'Hold up. We have all the time in the world for our souls to be together. Let's not burn out so quickly.' You understand?"

Oh God, Kathleen, please do not start on me, I said to myself. Seven-thirty-one p.m.

"Not really, Kathleen. But thanks anyway," I told her.

"Miramar," she said, putting down her knitting needles.

Here we go, I thought.

"Have you seen yourself lately? You're so skinny. You've got a whole set of luggage under your eyes. You walk around distracted all the time. You're always with him and when you're not, you're waiting for him. And I know you're not hitting the books anymore."

"I'm fine, Kathleen," I sighed, trying to sound casual.

"Listen. I know this is your first boyfriend. Take it from someone who has been to hell and back. If he's the one, go slow.... Don't make him think you're desperate for him. Keep him on his toes. Play it cool. Meanwhile, keep your eye out there just in case you miss The Love of Your Life. You know, your twin soul."

"Did you ever consider that he *is* my twin soul?" I scoffed at her, refusing to meet her eyes. *Click, click, click*. I knitted furiously now.

"Kitten, I am only trying to help," she sighed, returning to her yarn.

"I know, I know, Kathleen, but I'm not you." The phone rang. My heart paused.

"Let me, let me," she said. She languidly uncurled herself from her tangle of scarf. Hurry up, I wanted to scream.

"Hello? Hey, Jerry. How's it going? Oh, yah? Hahaha ... right, I know the one. Good times, good times.... Miramar? Hmmm ... let me see if she's around. That girl and her social life, you know. Always busy!" Kathleen held the receiver to her chest for one, two, three.... "Okay, she's right here. Hold on a sec." She handed the phone to me.

"Hi, Jerry. Where are you? The Market? Yes, that's the bar with the striped awning? Okay, I'll be there as soon as I can." The sun had risen and was shining on me again. I smiled at Kathleen as generously as I could before running to my room to put on some makeup. He loved me. I knew it.

Later that night, after another evening of pitchers, Jerry and I were in my bed. He was too drunk to have sex. I had to pull off his clothes and tuck him under the covers. Exhausted, I fell beside him. "Hey, Jerry?" I whispered.

"Hmmmm...." He mumbled from the pillow, his eyes already closed.

"How do you feel it's going? Like with us?"

"Whaaaa...?" He stretched his arms out in front of him and turned over to me with half-opened eyes.

"I love you," I whispered. I hated the unmistakable plead I heard in my voice.

A pause. "Thanks, Mir," he said, closing his eyes again and patting my arm. "Goodnight."

I lay in the darkness making excuses for his response — he

was tired, he was drunk, but the fear grew and spread through me like a snowstorm. As the flurries overcame my core, I trembled beneath the duvet, turning away from him and curling into myself.

Chapter 13 ⟿

The ancestors rely on the living to keep up their quality of life. They knew that without the requisite incense, paper money, and roast duck once in a while, prepare to have bad luck fall on your heads! The ancestors will curse you and suck their teeth about the ungrateful dogs that were their children. They will look hungrily at the other dead people whose children burned offerings and always remembered to put out a dish of meats and a can of Coke at the altar. The worst thing you can do to The Dead is to forget them.

As a frigid february blew in, as was planned what seemed a lifetime ago by three siblings who used to be one thing to each other but were now something else, I went home for the weekend of Chinese New Year. I hadn't seen my family in almost half a year. As the time neared, I thought about cancelling, sure that if I left Ottawa, Jerry would forget about me or find someone else. I imagined numerous scenarios in which women swarmed him like piranhas. But in the end, I kept my promise, and as the Greyhound neared Toronto, my eyes filled with tears.

Darwin shrieked when I came through the door and threw his arms around me, knocking me off balance. He had grown at least three inches since September.

"Let me take my coat off first, Dar," I laughed. He had on the round tortoiseshell glasses, a long-sleeved T-shirt with Yoda on it, and jeans.

"Hallo, Miramar Woo," he shouted. Darwin was always loud. "Wait 'til you see what I got you!" He dashed to his room. Ma came out of the kitchen, wiping her hands on her apron. She looked tired, with small half-moon shadows beneath her eyes, but her hair was neatly tied back, and she had a big smile across her small face.

"Miramar! Are you hungry?" she asked and patted me on the arm.

"Hi, Ma. You know what? I am hungry," I beamed back, still glowing from my little brother's enthusiasm. Ma took her cue and rushed back into the kitchen.

Darwin returned, skidding down the hallway, while I pulled off my boots. I noticed that Sophia was behind him. "Hey, Mir," she waved. Her hair was in a side ponytail tied with a bright pink scrunchie. I scooped her up in a big hug. My brother and sister felt so good to me; I had not realized how much I missed them.

Darwin shoved a small green bag, emblazoned with the gold label *Harrods* across it, at me. In his other hand, he held a long tube. "Ma helped me pick it out when we were in London," he said. I looked inside and pulled out a long box.

"Okay, okay, let me sit down," I laughed, going into the living room and settling on the couch while my siblings trailed after me.

"Open it, open it," Dar squealed. I flipped the box open. Inside, was an elegant fountain pen, with silver filigree covering its black body. I picked it up and was surprised at its heaviness. I took the cap off saw that its nib was engraved in gold and silver.

"Darwin, this is most beautiful pen I have ever seen," I exclaimed. Darwin jumped up and down.

"It's because you're a scholar, see? So you have to write some smart stuff with it, okay?"

"Okay, Dar, I will!" I laughed.

"I got Sophia the same thing, but in pencil, 'cause in math, you have to use an eraser." Of course, Sophia was the real scholar now. I felt a twinge.

Darwin gave me the tube next. "*Aiya,* let Miramar settle in," Ma called as she brought out a tray of food to the next room. We migrated to the dining-room table as Ma laid out congee and fried noodles. I sat, the table already set with my parents' good china and cloth napkins, and took out a poster of Boy George from the long tube.

"Look, look over here," Darwin pointed to the bottom left corner where Boy George's hand rested against his thigh. Scrawled in purple marker, it read, "Dear Darwin's sister. Your brother is a gas. Love, Boy George." I looked incredulously at Darwin, my mouth hanging open.

"He came to my performance at…" he looked at Ma. "Where were we, Ma?"

"Um. Name is Royal Albert," Ma replied as she ladled soup into small bowls.

"Yah, Boy George came to meet me backstage afterwards. He's pretty nice. He was in a dress! And makeup. He said we should record together sometime."

"Darwin, you are freaking amazing!" I hugged him and never wanted to let him go. Darwin shrugged. He was the same little brother he had always been whose best weapon was picking his nose and flicking it at people. He was also the same generous, lovely boy who always thought of others. Boy George had been lucky to meet Darwin Woo, I thought.

"Lemme go. You're squeezing me too hard," Darwin said, breathlessly. I released him even though I did not want to.

"Eat, *nui nui,* eat," Ma chided. She was calling me daughter, and it warmed me.

The rest of the visit was filled with their stories. Sophia described her colleagues at the Faculty of Mathematics at McGill, causing us to fall off our chairs laughing. She bent over and pretended to lean on a cane, crooning, "Class, class, you are about to witness brrrrilliance." She imitated each one of those men she called "The Dinosaurs." Ma pretended to be shocked at Sophia's insolence, saying she should respect her elders. Still, Ma couldn't resist laughing.

"But do you like them? Are they nice to you?" I asked.

"They're all right, I guess," Sophia sighed. "They're just so booooooring. And they always have food stains all over their clothes. Oh! And another thing. Their sweaters are like a million years old and covered in woolly pills. I want to shave them. You know how I can't stand that!" Sophia sneered.

"And the Gorkys?"

"Well, I love Mrs. Gorky. She's a real *artiste*. She paints watercolours and our house was done by a professional designer. It's truly rad."

"She feeds you enough, Sophia? You are too skinny," Ma frowned. "*Pai kwot mui*," she frowned. Skeleton girl.

"Yeah, Ma. We eat. We're vegetarians, Iris and I. She told me to call her Iris. Iris became a vegetarian because she says she couldn't hurt a fly so she couldn't justify eating a dead animal."

"Waaaa? You're not eating meat?" Ma wailed.

"No, Ma. Iris says there are some people who are vegetarian their whole lives and they're healthier than the rest of us. Iris says we are more spiritually attuned to the natural world when we don't have dead energy inside us. Meat is dead energy."

"*Tse-seene*," Ma proclaimed. Crazy. "Mrs. Gorky is wrong. You have to eat meat to stay healthy. *Tse-seene gwaipau*." Crazy ghost-lady.

"Well, I don't agree with you. Iris knows a lot more about it than you do." Sophia smiled tightly and examined her perfectly glossed pink fingernails.

Ma's face was turning purple. Hoping to derail Ma and Sophia from locking horns, I quickly turned to my brother who was sucking up a noodle, his head over his bowl. "Darwin, how are the people you're living with?"

He shrugged. "S'okay."

"S'okay? It's very nice. The nicest residence," Ma said.

Darwin nodded. "It's pretty cool. I got a new Atari 7800 in my room."

"And the conservatory? Are you having fun there?"

"It's okay. A lot of rehearsals. Sometimes, I just want to sleep, but they wake us up at six a.m. to be in class for seven-thirty. Torture."

"Do you have friends?" I continued to push him for more glimpses of his life in London.

"Yeah. There's a guy two years older than me there from Brazil. His name is Raul. He's a prodigy too. He likes *Pac-Man*."

This made me happy. Thank God for Raul, another freak genius in the world so that my brother would not be alone.

On New Year's night, we chatted and ate our dinner of steamed clams, broccoli and beef in black bean sauce, and roast duck. I suspected Sophia had only become a convenient vegetarian because she dived into everything and had seconds. We continued to catch up like people who had gone on separate vacations when Sophia suddenly said, "I'd like to visit Ba."

We looked at Ma. She laid down her chopsticks and looked into her bowl a long time before she finally answered in forceful Cantonese, "We do not talk of the dead on Chinese New Year."

"But I'm only here for a short time. I want to go to the grave," Sophia persisted. Things had been going so smoothly. Ma had even included a dish of simmered tofu and vegetables as a goodwill gesture for Sophia.

"We will not talk of the dead," Ma said again in the same cold even tone.

"You mean we should never talk about Ba now? Because with the way things are going, and how hectic our schedules are, we'll only see each other during the New Year," Sophia's voice started to get whiny. I felt the familiar gathering of winds that always marked the beginning of battle between Ma and Sophia.

We weren't done eating, but Ma stood and started to clear the plates, her head down.

"Did you hear me, Ma? Hello? I asked you a question," Sophia persisted. I kicked her under the table.

"Ouch!" Sophia shot me a drop-dead look.

Ma went to the kitchen with her first load of dirty dishes.

"Stop it, Sophia," I hissed. "Just stop. It's too soon for her. Leave it alone."

"Not for me. I want to go," Sophia answered. Darwin looked down at the table.

"Then you go. You go alone, okay? Or I'll go with you. Just drop it."

Sophia flung herself back in her chair and crossed her arms. "Am I the only one who remembers Ba around here? Shit!"

Ma came around the corner and slammed her hands on the table. We jumped. "You think you're the only one? You're the only one who lost Ba? You think so?" Ma's voice rose.

Sophia didn't answer. Something in Ma's eyes told me this was different, not like any of their other fights.

"You know nothing! Nothing!" Ma thrust a finger in Sophia's face. Her whole body was trembling.

I got up from the table. "I'll help clean up, Ma. Don't worry about this." I waved my hand around the table, meaning the dishes, but what I really meant was the whole thing with Sophia, even though I knew that was impossible. My heart was speeding up.

Ma sat down, looking as if the air had been let out of her. The only sound was the dishes clinking together as I stacked them. "No talking about the dead on the New Year," she repeated in a voice so quiet it sent shivers down my back. She turned to face the photo of Ba that was now hung on the wall. I didn't understand what was happening. She could look at him, think about him while seeing his face, but we couldn't talk about him. I had to side with Sophia then, and wonder why not? He loved New Year. We were here for him.

Sophia stood up and pushed her chair against the table roughly. "Fine. Thanks very much. Great to see ya, Ma, as usual," she said and went to her room.

Ma kept to her seat, her eyes still on the photo of Ba. It was the one of him taken on a fishing trip in High Park. He was laughing, squinting in the sun, a tiny perch attached to his hook. I remember the *gweilos* had stared at us. No one else had been fishing. I guessed that for them, the pond was just decoration: a small synthetic lake in the middle of their city park. But for Ba, it had been a fishing hole. I watched Ma as she looked at the photo, unable to read in her face what she was thinking. I sat down beside her while Darwin kept his eyes on the table.

"*Mo baun fat,*"Ma whispered. No solution.

"To what, Ma?" I asked her, wondering if I should hold her hand or touch her, something I knew people did when someone they loved was hurting. I must have taken too long to consider because she got up and went to her room before I could move.

Sophia re-emerged a couple of hours later to join Darwin and me in the living room. We were about to watch the final episode of *The Wonder Years*.

"Move over, little D," Sophia nudged Darwin, and he shuffled over on the couch. Sophia snuggled in, one arm around Darwin. I was on the other side of him, reaching my arm across his shoulders too. Our Ba's matching La-z-Boy, in the same brown-and-gold floral pattern as our couch, sat empty.

We watched the show silently. We had watched Kevin Arnold grow up and made deep philosophical connections about life with his pals, Paul and Winnie. The final episode ended with a quote from the adult Kevin as the camera rose above the neighbourhood and flew over it: "I remember a place, a town, a house like a lot of houses. A yard like a lot of yards, on a street like a lot of other streets. And the thing is, after all these years, I still look back ... with wonder."

I pulled Darwin closer, his small frame contoured around mine. Sophia drew closer and the three of us fit like jigsaw pieces in a puzzle. Something about Kevin's final words as the credits rolled lingered. I choked back tears as I felt something intangible had just gotten lost and was irretrievable.

Chapter 14 ⌁

*Mei Mei never said very much. Her deeds spoke louder than words.
She cooked her man his food, tended to his wounds when the bandits came to pillage his village, and hung his laundry. She died from
a mysterious disease that robbed her of her life but did not diminish
her goodness. It was a lovely death as she died in his arms. He wept,
vowing he would never love again, that he was not worthy of Mei Mei.
But he actually did find love again, and quickly, with a horseback-riding
female outlaw who could sword fight. Mei Mei observed all this in the
afterlife and told her beloved to go fuck himself.*

IN APRIL, SUMMER ARRIVED in Ottawa pretty well bypassing
spring. That winter had stretched on and on. The hot weather
sizzled away the snow, and people went from snowsuits to
shorts in a matter of weeks.

When the school term ended, I decided to stick around. I had
barely passed my courses and figured I would attend summer
school. The row of Ds in my transcript looked like a firing
squad. I had never gone below a B before. Rigorous girlfriend
training took a lot out of me, but now that I had gotten the
hang of it, I figured my grades would bounce back.

Of course, if my family had said to come home, I would
have been on the next bus, but after I spoke to them, I saw
there wouldn't be much of a home to go home to for summer.
After McGill's term ended, Sophia left straight away to spend
a few weeks at a summer institute for child geniuses in New

York, and Darwin was booked to go on some "Wonders of the World" tour with the London Philharmonic Orchestra. Over the next few weeks, I received snapshots, mailed like postcards, of Darwin wearing different *Star Wars* T-shirts, each with a message from him on the back. He spent the space of each card theorizing how the sites reminded him of specific characters: The Great Wall of China was Darth Vader because China was a little like the Death Star; he wore Princess Leia at the Taj Mahal, because out of all the sites, he wrote, "This one was the most 'girly'"; in the one of him in front of the Great Pyramid of Giza, he was wearing Yoda: "Obviously," he wrote, "because this is the oldest of the great wonders *and* the one with the most mysterious powers"; and then there was the requisite Luke Skywalker featured in the photo of Dar looking like he was holding up the Leaning Tower of Pisa. "D'uh," he scrawled, "it's a light saber." He signed each photo with, *May the force be with you, Darwin Woo.*

Ma had gone back to Toronto alone. She said the conservatory had assigned Darwin a legal guardian to accompany him on his tour. I supposed that I should have gone home to keep her company, but she seemed content with church and *mah jong* and good-deed-doing. I waited, even tried to subtly prompt her, but she never asked me to return.

Before Chinese New Year, my phone calls with Ma had been short, always beginning with her asking me if I was eating. She told me about her *mah jong* games, especially if she won big. Some gossip about her friends, like how Mrs. Chu's daughter brought home a girlfriend to a family dinner, and short updates on Darwin and Sophia, rounded out the few minutes. But after New Years, we called each other even less — first, it was every couple of weeks, then monthly, and then only occasionally. I could have picked up the phone and called more often, but something always stopped me. Memories of our last Chinese New Year dinner lingered, and I was afraid of stirring up what lay beneath Ma's surface.

Jerry didn't mind going home for the summer; in fact, he left for a construction job in North Bay even before his classes were over. I got a receptionist job at the university's Counselling Centre, then moved out of the Amityville House and into a bachelor apartment closer to downtown. Jerry said he would visit one weekend each month and, in my mind, I condensed the summer and pictured my life with Jerry come fall; of course, he would stay over a lot during the next school year, almost like we were living together. I sensed Kathleen was hurt at my hasty departure, but an invisible wedge had developed between us ever since she had said I was getting too serious with Jerry.

On the phone, he sounded so far away. "Why don't I come visit you? You know, you can show me the bush," I teased.

"No, Mir. I don't want youse to have to meet my dad. The fucking asshole. There's nowhere for you to stay."

The pain he was in, and the difficulty of his family, made Jerry seem that much more deserving of my love. The more he suffered, the more I swooned. At first, we talked nightly. Then the calls came weekly. Jerry said he was so drained from the work that he often fell asleep right after dinner. I imagined giving him back rubs, cooking him dinner, stroking his calloused hands.

But then he just didn't call. He said he would, but the call never came. A week went by. Two. Then June came and went. Despite the terrible heat that had overtaken Ottawa, I felt as cold as I had been when Ba died. I longed for his sweaters. As the days rolled on, I couldn't think about anything else but Jerry. I started making mistakes at the Counselling Centre, like double-booking the appointments.

I didn't know how to contact him. He had never left a number at his father's house, and I would be too scared to call him there anyway. Jerry could be dead, in a ditch, under a rock, lost in the river. I knew North Bay was a wild place. Perhaps he had been reclaimed by the wild; his corpse probably covered in a mossy grave, or being fed on by big-mouthed bass, morsel by morsel. My morbid imagination ran in circles; I was haunted by images of Jerry's body, blue and lifeless on a bed of dried pine needles. I actually took comfort in the image of a dead Jerry. It was less painful than the alternatives: Jerry forgetting me, Jerry cheating on me, Jerry being too busy for me.

Finally, one humid night in July, my phone rang past midnight. I was in my pajamas and in bed. The sweat rained down my face as I listened to Jerry's voice. It began badly. "Sorry, Miramar. I'm really sorry. I love youse. Youse may not believe me, but it's true. I've never said it, but you're too intense, girl. I didn't want youse to take it the wrong way. It's better that you're there and I'm here. Finish school. Do something with your life."

"What the hell are you talking about?" My heart thudded loudly. I wondered if he could hear it. "You're breaking up with me?"

"Like I said. Things are complicated. I've got work here, and I hardly pulled the grades to go into second year anyway. So, it's just better for me to stay here. I mean, what I mean is ... shit! Listen, you belong elsewhere. In like a big city or something. Back in Toronto. You're gonna finish school and do great things. Me, I don't belong anywhere but back here."

His speech was impassioned, drunken, full of all the emotion I had been so craving from him, and all of it too late. It hit me, it hit hard. I sealed my eyes and some tears ran into my temples. "You're seeing someone else." I said. I knew the answer even as I waited. The silence was like a million spiders crawling up my leg. "Just fucking tell me!" I screamed into the phone.

"Um. Yah. I started seeing an old girlfriend from high school. We just sorta hooked up again. She's more like me, ya know. We belong here. My dad kicked me out, and Sheryl let me stay with her. She's been like, there for me." Another long silence trailed behind his words. I felt like throwing up.

"And yah, so that's it. It's not you, Mir. Honestly. We're just too different. And I just ... I don't know. I just can't."

I clutched the phone until my knuckles drained of blood. I
didn't know what else to say. Plead? Beg?

"So, that's it. I hope youse get everything you want 'cause
youse deserve it. You're one of the best people I know."

I suddenly realized how much I hated it when Jerry referred
to me as "youse."

The heartbreak was too much. I blasted Cyndi Lauper's
"Time After Time" from my boombox and retreated into a
shell so thick it made my invisibility act in high school seem
like amateur hour. None of it made sense. People said they
loved you, but then they left. Either I was missing some kind
of fundamental logic about the human condition, or Jerry
was just a liar. Both were plausible. Or, the world was just a
mess of accidents colliding. Ba's death, the hands haunting
Ma, The Gifts, and my ordinariness — all of it random and
uninvited.

The pain of being let go seeped into me like slow poison. I
had already been here, and this time felt twice as bad. I forced
myself to get out of bed, to go to work, to go home, to eat, to
sleep, then rinse and repeat. Inside, the pain pooled and grew,
and I could only take sharp shallow breaths in order not to
suffocate.

At work, after all the counsellors had gone home, I started
reading the client files. They were just like *True Confessions*
magazine but better. I felt calmer reading about others' crises.
There was a beautiful girl who came once a week to see one
of the counsellors at the Centre. She had everything going for
her that signified how the world could be so generous: long
blond hair, bright blue eyes, long slim legs to her teeth, and a
bedazzling smile. And she was nice. Like, really, really nice.
She always asked me how I was, as if she was waiting for a
pedicure instead of her therapist. I found out from her file that
she was sleeping with her father.

Another client was a skinny mute boy named Daniel who carried around a pad of paper. When he would arrive for his appointment, he would flip to the first page that had written on it in neat print: Daniel Greyeyes. I loved his name and a glance at his face confirmed that his eyes were indeed the colour of dawn. Every time he came in, he presented me with one of the pages of his notebook. I would confirm his appointment and ask him to have a seat. He would flip to "Thank you." The other pages held different words: "yes," "no," "maybe," "later," "now," his address, his phone number, the number "19," which I guessed was his age. While he sat in the waiting room, he slowly leafed through the pad. I peered at him from behind the file cabinets, pretending to work. There were also pencil sketches, doodles, and scraps of paper stapled to the pages.

Apparently, he was referred to the Counselling Centre by the administration. His dorm rep had written up a report, citing that Daniel was not adjusting well to university life. He seemed isolated, it said. His roommate claimed he spent all of his time alone in their room, flipping through his notebook. He was failing all his courses because he didn't hand in any assignments or show up for exams. Counselling was part of his academic probation. His counsellor, Louis, wrote little in his file.

Soon Daniel Greyeyes stopped showing up for his appointments. His counsellor handed me his file one day and said I should file it with the other "Dormant" files in the cabinet. Instead, I slipped the file into my bag and took it home. It was a swift, decisive move, despite the fact that I didn't know what made me do it. In the last entry, Louis wrote that Daniel had officially withdrawn from the university. That was all it said. I ripped a piece of lined paper from my binder and printed in block letters: "GOODBYE," and inserted it into his file.

Throughout the rest of the summer I swiped other "Dormant" files. Janeanne Blix committed suicide after months of depression. Lee Smithers compulsively ate himself to over 500 pounds and couldn't get out of the house for appointments. Theresa Falango, who had been raised in a cult, made delicate criss-cross patterns on her arms with razor blades. She also disappeared and never returned to the office. I collected them all, placing them in a banker's box underneath my desk at home. Late at night, when I couldn't sleep, I took them out, read them again, and wondered if there was one thing that someone could have done to change the course of events in each of their lives.

The summer passed by achingly. I didn't see anyone except for the counsellors and their clients. After work, I stopped by the corner store, returned to my square box of a room, ate a pint of rocky road ice cream for dinner and settled in front of the TV until I fell into a chocolate marshmallow coma. Kathleen called to check in once in a while, but I never felt like going out.

"Kitten, you have to snap out of this. Jerry was just one fish in the big wide sea. C'mon, cheer up," Kathleen would coax. I knew she meant well, but I could not bear the thought that there was some self-satisfaction in her voice. She had known this would happen. She had tried to ready me for it. Fuck her.

The grief was like an avalanche that grew stronger and more powerful each day. I could not get up. I lay there and let the rocks run over me.

Chapter 15 ⌒

The Snake Sisters were immortals who lived for thousands of years and protected humans from ill fate — one was Green, the other White. They stopped floods from destroying villages and grew herbs to heal those who suffered from plague. They also mastered slipping into human form, passing as beautiful women who had suitors up the wazoo. Green Snake was the bold one who thirsted for adventure. She saw humans only as her playthings. White Snake respected mortals and fell in love with a scholar until Green Snake blew their cover and scared him to death by mistakenly revealing her reptilian self. This began a thousand-year feud.

IN THE MIDDLE OF AUGUST, Sophia came for a visit. The Gorkys had gone to Paris on holiday, and Sophia was miffed they had not take her along. I wondered whether she had considered going to visit Ma, but I suspected, since she was coming to stay with me rather than going home to Toronto, that things were not okay between them.

When she entered my apartment, she looked surprised. "Where's the rest of it?" she asked, not jokingly.

I threw down her duffle bag, closed the door behind us, and sighed. Princess Sophia had landed. "This is it," I said. Sophia turned to look me, really look at me since the taxi had deposited her at the door. I did not miss the head-to-toe scan and I knew exactly what she saw. I had lost one of the contact lenses down the drain and had gone back to wearing my giant round glasses that she had always said made me look like an owl. I was sadly in need of a haircut, and looked like Cousin It. My chin was dotted with acne. I had also gained weight, but I had squeezed myself into my acid-washed jeans because I wanted to look at least half-okay for my sister.

Sophia, in a red leather mini-skirt, black V-neck T-shirt, and strappy sandals, her nails perfectly groomed in pearly pink, looked like she was ready for a photo shoot. I tugged at my oversized T-shirt and tucked it in. Standing beside my sister, I always felt like a garden gnome.

Sophia turned to the empty ice cream cartons overflowing in the garbage, the unmade bed, the client files strewn across the floor. She opened the refrigerator and the cold empty shelves hummed back at us. She turned to me while I half-heartedly attempted to make the bed. "Mir, you are getting the money, right?"

"Yes. I'm getting the money." I tossed the comforter and let it fall flat. Ba had always made sure his life insurance was up-to-date, so I was getting a healthy allowance from his estate. Ma was also sending some of the money Sophia and Darwin earned from their public appearances and work. This made me feel worse than horrible. I could not bear to touch it, so every dime I had received sat in my account accumulating interest, which I planned to return to them one day. "Why are you asking?" I smoothed down the bed cover.

"Well, you have no food. You look like shit. I don't know. Something's wrong," Sophia replied.

"I'm okay. I just forgot to do the groceries. I didn't know what you wanted." I fluffed up the pillows.

"Uh, okay. But you still look like shit." Sophia started unpacking and looking around at the bare flat to see where she could put her clothes.

"Gee, thanks. It's nice to see you too," I scowled. I did not need Sophia to come and shake me out of my slump. I was just beginning to get comfortable there.

"Well, I can't live like this," she said and bent over to start picking up the client files from the floor. Seeing her touching my files made me feel as though she had grabbed my heart with her bare hands. "Don't touch those!" I shrieked. Sophia dropped them, startled. I scrambled over to them and gathered them to my chest. I took the stack and put them in the boxes beneath my desk. "Sorry, it's just that those are for work. They're really important documents."

"Riiiight," Sophia replied and started in on the garbage bag instead. It was not a big place. Twelve-by-twelve feet of living. We had it cleaned up in less than twenty minutes. Sophia gave up trying to unpack when she realized there really wasn't anywhere for her to put her things. She laid her bag back on the floor and flopped onto the bed, the only place to sit besides the desk chair. I lay down beside her and stared at the light fixture in the ceiling. Sophia reached for my hand. I realized I hadn't felt another person's touch since Jerry. A tear slid down the side of my face. She pushed my dirty hair aside and said, "Spill, sister."

I hadn't talked to anyone, like really talked, in a long time. I looked at Sophia, her familiar face. I thought, why not? There was nothing left for me to lose. So I unloaded. I told her how much I had liked it here at first, how exciting it all was. I loved my classes, all the people I was meeting. For the first time, I felt normal. Like maybe I wasn't destined to be a geek, a loser, the shy kid forever. I felt like I belonged, not in the corner, but front and centre. Then I told her about Jerry right up to the break-up that had bulldozed all that over.

"It sucks," I confessed. Sophia reached her arms around me. Being vulnerable with her was new territory in our relationship, and I felt naked. But now, we were alone in the world, and maybe it was becoming like Ba had told us when we were little, "One for all and all for Woo!" He had said that we should always stick up for each other because nothing was more important than family. I used to think he was corny whenever he made that big pronouncement, but sitting here with my sister, I didn't think that anymore.

"I miss him, Soph," I said from beneath my mass of greasy hair.

She snorted. "You'll get over that jerk. He's not good enough for you. Some dickwad from North Bay. Where the hell is that anyway?"

"No, Ba, I miss Ba," I whispered. There was a long silence.

Sophia leaned her head on my shoulder. "Yeah. So do I, Mir. So do I." We stayed like that for a long time.

"Hey, I know what'll cheer you up." Sophia suddenly sat upright.

I sat up too. I hoped she wasn't going to suggest going to the mall. But I could see it burning in her eyes in a way that softened me. It was such a comfort to know someone so well. Then I didn't mind anymore. Maybe I would even enjoy buying something.

Later that night over takeout chicken wings, Sophia told me about life in Montreal. We sat cross-legged on the floor while we ate. Sophia had even bought flowers at the grocery store and arranged them in a jam jar between us. The chicken wings spilled out on a foil wrapper along with various sauces in small Styrofoam containers.

"We always have fresh flowers at home. Mrs. Gorky ... I mean, Iris, tells me it's all in the details. A room is naked until adorned with flowers. She talks like that all the time. I get a kick out of her. Her whole life is about being a faculty wife. She has the best dinner parties, the nicest house, and the best manners. And, oh my God, she's beautiful. Mir, I hope I look like her when I'm fifty-eight. She's got this brown hair, but with a streak of white on the left side. Like, wow. What a statement. She always dresses impeccably. She doesn't try to dress like she's younger or older. Somehow she gets it right, ya know?" I really had no idea, but I nodded.

"Anyway, no one knows that she's bulimic. I know, because I hear her barfing when she doesn't think I'm home. It's pretty gross. She acts like she has it all, but she's actually really lonely. Professor Gorky is nice and all, but all he thinks about is math. That's all he talks to me about. Meanwhile, Iris couldn't balance the cheque-book if her life depended on it. But he doesn't know she's unhappy, see? Because she doesn't show it. He thinks they're great. Better than great. He's got the wife everybody in his department adores. He doesn't see anything wrong. One day though, something's gonna give. You watch." Sophia waved her chicken wing in the air to emphasize her point. She dipped it in honey and garlic sauce and nibbled.

"I think I'm going to convert. Become Jewish. Iris thinks I should too. I go to synagogue with her all the time, we observe the Sabbath, so like, what's the big deal. I may as well just make it official."

"What? Okay, back up," I exclaimed. Sophia had the irritating habit of switching topics suddenly.

"Why not? Chinese people can be Jews. Did you know there's a whole colony of Chinese Jews in China?" Sophia had a smidge of sauce on the corner of her mouth. "Benjamin told me that."

"Who's Benjamin?" I asked. She poked a wing into the sour cream. I didn't say anything, waiting for Sophia to elaborate.

"Okay. I have a boyfriend. He's the Gorkys' son. He's also married. And he's thirty-two," Sophia replied.

"Sophia Woo, what the hell?" I screamed. Sophia's gall never ceased to amaze me.

"That's the bad news. The good news is he's goooorgeous. He looks like that lead singer of the Thompson Twins, only better. He's funny and smart. Like, really smart. Not math geek smart. God knows I meet enough of those nerds. He's cool. Ben's wife travels a lot for business. She's never there. The witch. Can you believe leaving your husband for weeks at a time?" Sophia was breathless from pouring out all that information. I could tell she had practiced telling me about

Benjamin. Sophia was very convincing and organized when she wanted to persuade you to her side. She hit on the the bad points first, then the good points.

"And Ben thinks my eyes are beautiful. Not weird or deformed. He's so nice, huh?" Sophia was paddling as fast as she could. My mouth remained as wide open as her eyes. Exasperated, she exploded, "God, Miramar! Say something!"

I didn't know what to say. I continued to stare into my sister's skewed eyes, seeing the pleading there. "But you're just a kid…" I sputtered. "That's rape." Sophia sighed angrily.

"I'm not a friggin' kid. Hell, I lecture. At a university. Look, just be happy for me, okay? I can't tell anyone else. You're the only one. So at least be happy that I'm happy."

"How can you be happy? The guy's like, an adult. A married-with-children adult. Where do you think this is going?"

"Who cares where it's going. I'm happy. Now is all we have. At least I have one person in Montreal who doesn't treat me like some prized dog or freak of nature," Sophia replied hotly.

"How can you think like that? You're going to get hurt," I continued, hearing the echo of Kathleen as I said this. I bit my bottom lip.

"Like I said, all we have is now. So who cares? He says he loves me. And, I like him. A lot." Her sentence hung in the air, adding to the electricity between us.

Sophia always jumped before knowing what pile she was going to land in. But at least, I was reluctant to admit, she always landed on her feet. It seemed Sophia had always been like this, stubborn, refusing to listen to reason once she had decided on something. Ba had let her get away with a lot, even when I knew he hadn't approved. Like, he hadn't liked her wearing all those ripped-up jeans. He had worked hard so we could look respectable, but he let it go when Sophia took her scissors to every pair she had.

"Are you going to tell Ma?" I asked, already knowing this would make Sophia edgier than she already was.

"Oh my God, Miramar. She'd send me for an exorcism or something. Besides Ma is busy with her own life." Before I could protest, she continued, "Ma doesn't want to come to Montreal. Since Chinese New Year, she hardly calls me anymore. She doesn't give a shit about me, and frankly, I don't care." I knew Sophia too well to believe her. Her face was screwed up, but I couldn't tell whether it was from anger or loss.

"Anyway," she paused dramatically, "I think she's seeing someone."

"Whaaaaaaaaa?"

"I don't know. I talked to Darwin the other night, and he said Ma went to visit him in London, and that she told him she had a new friend — a man friend."

I shook my head to make sure I was hearing clearly. Was this some distraction tactic of Sophia's to get me to shut up about her affair?

"It's just speculation on your part," I said.

"Is not."

"Is."

"Is not."

"Shut up, Sophia. I swear you drive me friggin' crazy!" I finally yelled.

"Whatever," she shrugged. "You always want to believe what you want to believe."

"What is that supposed to mean?" I asked. Just when I thought we had matured into friends, she had to go pushing my buttons.

"I mean you're a gullible child who just wants to believe everything is fine. Meanwhile, things aren't fine. Even with this stupid North Bay Jerry. You sit around pretending you're okay when you're not. If it were me, I would have taken the bus to North Freaking Bay to find out what was going on waaaay before he broke up with me. But you just let things happen. You're always like that. You act like you don't have a choice or something. You know what, Miramar? You're not shy; you're just scared." She pointed her finger into my chest. "*You* are a chicken shit. That's what you are," Sophia spewed.

I felt like she had stabbed me.

"Oh, God, don't look at me like that. Shit, Miramar. Don't be such a victim. Grow the fuck up." Sophia got up and shut herself in the washroom.

I couldn't help how I looked. I crawled into my bed and buried my head into the pillow.

We didn't bring Benjamin or Ma up again during Sophia's visit, but the intimacy we had forged in the beginning fell away like a discarded blanket. Sophia could go from purring like a cat against your leg one moment, to throwing poisonous darts in a manner of seconds. The world through Sophia's crossed eyes was divided into two groups: for her or against her.

Knowing this, I tried to win back Sophia's favour with more trips to the Rideau Centre. I even let her pick out clothes for me, stuff I would not wear in a million years, but the cord of tension stayed in the air throughout the rest of her visit.

Her words had stung. I heard them reverberating in my brain a million times. It should have been me who was giving her the chilly treatment. The fragile thread that had always kept us tied to one other seemed frayed, and the ends tangled. But that last night, I felt so comforted by her light snore as if it were the most soothing music. I had slept next to that snore for most of my life. I didn't realize how much I had relied on it for a peaceful night of sleep.

When Sophia left, I stood on the platform and waved until I could no longer see the Montreal-bound train. Although I was relieved to be allowed back into my downward spiral, I felt the ground grow soft beneath my feet as I watched the train disappear.

Chapter 16 ⌒

When her village was captured, the barbarians thought Lan was too ugly to take as a wife so they made her collect rocks to make them a new fort. One day, she found a green ribbon in the rubble. Lan knew it had belonged to the pretty merchant's daughter who used to tie back her long raven hair. Lan used to envy her for this ribbon, something she could never hope to afford. The merchant's daughter now lay dead in a ditch in the woods. Lan tied the ribbon into her own matted hair. The barbarians laughed at her, thinking this was a vain attempt to be pretty, but they did not know that Lan was wearing it in tribute.

THAT FALL, I WENT BACK to classes a different person, cleaner somehow, like someone who had been scrubbed raw. I let myself get lost in books, a far safer refuge than people. Feminist Ideas. Philosophy of Eastern Religion. Sociolinguistics. Abnormal Psychology. Mass Communications. I had to drop out of Journalism since my first-year grades were so bad, so I opted for Sociology, an easy option with many multiple-choice exams. Besides, Sociology intrigued me. People, clustered together, needing each other, hating each other, defining themselves in and out of groups — at last, I learned that there were many ways of making sense of this mess we called humankind.

One afternoon in November, feeling cabin fever in my tiny apartment and craving instant noodles, I burst out into the crisp air to Chinatown. Ottawa's version was only one main street cutting through three little blocks. The leaves were falling again, but this time I was indifferent to Ottawa's beauty. The smell of the late autumn decay, which last year had soothed and excited me, now just felt gloomy and sad.

I walked by a video store and saw Jackie Chan in a poster of *Drunken Master* taped to the window. I had always loved that movie. My tired heart suddenly ached for Ba.

I went in and rented the classic, returning for armloads more as the days passed. In my apartment, I replicated the moves. *They* were all wrong about me; I was Miramar Woo, woman warrior of the west. Between spoonfuls of ice cream, I was whooping crane, praying mantis, lethal sword. "*Heeeeeyaaaa,*" I would cry, then perform my best roundhouse kick.

As for my enemies, if they were not evil warlords, then it was Jerry. I kicked him in the nuts with a quick front kick, and slammed his head with a narrow, penetrating strike. I imagined standing over his limp body while he apologized and vowed ever-lasting loyalty to me. Alone in my fantasy world, my heart raced. I felt alive! Certainly more alive than I felt in my real life. I was beginning to worry that I was turning into one of those Dungeon and Dragons geeks in high school who would bring their little figures to school and play in the cafeteria. Even I had thought they were freaks. But now, I was realizing I could be the biggest freak of all. At least the D&D boys had each other. I was entirely alone.

I continued working at the Counselling Centre until one day, when the Director asked me to come to his office. I sat across from him and glanced around at my surroundings while he finished a phone call: I saw silk flowers, a small aquarium with two fish, a porcelain teacup painted with delicate pink roses and a gold rim, a marble pen holder. Neutral, contemplative objects. A large window overlooked the river. I was sure he had curated this place to be as nonthreatening as possible.

He hung up and after some idle *gweilo* chit-chat, he asked,

"So, Miramar, we seem to be missing some files. The 'Dormant' cases? Do you know anything about that?"

I looked right into his pink, fleshy face. "No, doctor, I don't."

"It's the most curious thing. A number of them have gone missing. *Poof.* Just like that." He snapped his fingers loudly.

I forced my face to relax. "Sorry."

"Oh, well," he sighed. "If you could please keep a lookout for them, I would appreciate it."

"You bet," I said cheerily, and stood up. Then, I turned around and made my feet move slowly, casually, surprised by how easy it was to lie. I was proud of myself.

"Oh, and Miramar."

"Yes." I swivelled back to face him.

"How are you doing? Are you okay?" he asked, still in his seat. He took his glasses off. "I just want to check in from time to time. You know, it's what we *do.*" He smiled, and it seemed sincere. The kind of smile that made me want to sit back down and actually tell him things. I opened my mouth a little and considered just letting it all fly out, but in that long pause, he had returned to the papers on his desk. So I left.

A few days later, I quit the job, using a heavy course load as an excuse. I felt it was my obligation to keep the files safe. The files helped me remember to stay on the right side of the abyss in front of me. I felt responsible for all the people in those files, and I believed if I kept them close, I could keep them from being forgotten. I thought briefly about making an altar to the files, someplace where I could stick an orange and a Sprite, but decided that gesture was too final. The people in these files were not all dead; they were just on pause. But they needed to be acknowledged. If their suffering was real to me, then they would not be alone in it.

Chapter 17

Feast days were important rituals to bind family together. Favoured animals were sacrificed and charred to perfection, the menus were planned weeks in advance, the balance restored as sweetness chased out all the bitterness of the past. In food, lies this hope.

THE WINTER OF '89, I went back to Toronto for Chinese New Year. If I had any feelings about it, I didn't let myself feel them. Ma had moved into a new condo downtown. She only told me after the fact. She said some real estate agent friend from church suggested she try it out before selling the house and moving somewhere new, so he had loaned it to her. At the time, I had wondered briefly about this — where do real estate agents get apartments they can just loan out? But what I knew about real estate was nothing, so I had simply let it go. She had left our house. That was the larger issue.

When I asked her why, she had just said, "Aw, *nui*, the house is too big just for me. Anyway, the condo is very nice. Easy. No need to shovel snow. Everything clean."

Anyone else would be glad for Ma. Good for her, they would say. She deserved a rest. She had worked hard keeping up the house. But while our house was firmly rooted in the earth, surrounded by trees and anchored by lawn and sidewalk, I was instantly disoriented walking into this airy place with its cold marble lobby and security guard behind a granite counter. And the condo was so high up it seemed disconnected from the earth as if it were on a shelf in the clouds. The living room, dining room, and kitchen were all one big space thrust against the large window that looked out onto Lake Ontario. And because it came fully furnished with a pristine leather sectional, a teak coffee table, and a glass dining-room table with matching chairs, no trace of our past was in evidence. If Ma had been difficult to know before she inhabited this white cube, now in such a sterile context, she was a stranger.

Then again, maybe it was just me who was the stranger. I had been so preoccupied with myself that I had not considered Ma for a long time. Maybe she was finally feeling happy and needed to shed some of her old life — our old life — to heal and move forward. Maybe the house was too full of Ba.

While I had let my own appearance fall into shambles, Ma looked like a teenager. Her long black hair was tied back in a ponytail. Her unlined face was bright and clear. I showed up that morning for New Year, like I did to every day of my life, in my Roots sweatpants and matching sweatshirt. Ma answered the door in an A-line denim skirt that grazed her knee and a cowl-necked top with an image of a silver Eiffel tower on the front. And lipstick, which I had never seen her wear before. From my memory of Kathleen's cosmetic teachings, I thought it looked like Revlon's "Plum Pudding."

At least she greeted me sounding like her old self. "Miramar, what's wrong? Are you sick? Do you need some *dong gui* soup? Are you getting your period?" Ma asked before moving back into the kitchen.

I supposed I was still dragging my heart around the floor like a soggy mop, my sadness growing in proportion to my waistline. Ma's look of concern sank me further into a mudhole.

"Yah, Ma. I'm fine. Just put on a little weight, that's all." I looked at the cream carpet. There were a million things about this condo and Ma that startled me. In our previous life, Ma would never have approved of anything as impractical as a light carpet. "*Aiya*. Too easy to see the dirt!" she would have said. I felt angry with this woman whom I barely recognized. Was life so much better for her now that Ba was dead? Maybe Sophia was right that Ma had a man. I had been fretting all this time about Ma's mental stability, but meanwhile this new woman was emerging and she seemed, well, she seemed better.

I stared at her back. Seeing her looking so lovely, her words so crisp and bright, I felt relieved. Here was Ma seeming healthy, happy, and offering to make me an herbal remedy so I could feel better. I was overwhelmed by the tangle of emotions.

"Aw. You study too much, *nui*. Take it easy. I worry," Ma said. She reached out her hand as if to brush my overgrown bangs out of my face, but I pulled back and she dropped it before it reached my skin. I could not bear the thought of her hand on me. If she did touch me, I thought, I felt like I would fall down and die. I hadn't been touched by anyone in a long time, not since Sophia, and I still remembered how that had turned out.

We spent an awkward afternoon alone together, not knowing what to say. Mainly, Ma had kept her back to me while she chopped at the counter and stirred at the stove. I realized that without Ba, we didn't know how to fill in the silence. Luckily, Sophia's arrival was like a hundred bees home to hive. She had just come back from a trigonometry conference at Berkeley, and was dressed from head-to-toe in lime green. She had woven plastic flowers in her new asymmetrical bobbed hair in an ode to San Francisco. She swept Ma and me up in a dramatic hug and raved to Ma about the condo. According to Sophia, it was *trés* chic.

As I helped her unpack in the bedroom, Sophia announced in a stage whisper that she had a new boyfriend named Derek.

"Benjamin turned out to be a complete loser," Sophia claimed. "He broke it off with me after his wife decided she was through with travelling and took up a desk job in Montreal. Derek, on the other hand, is *scrumptious*," she said, quickly skipping over this gap. "You'll be happy, Mir. He's only twenty-one, five years older." She paused meaningfully. She did not bring up the tension of our last visit, and I wasn't going to either. "I met him at the *Tête-à-Tête*, a sandwich joint on St. Laurent Boulevard."

According to Sophia, he was the six-foot-three version of Prince. Elegantly androgynous and thoroughly francophone, she loved the Jheri curls that hung out of his hairnet while he made her a *croque-monsier*. He adored her franglish. He was, appropriately, a musician. An experimental Acid Jazz saxophonist to be exact. The sandwich gig was just to allow him to continue his craft.

"He has great lips," Sophia asserted. "But don't tell Ma," she added, pretending to turn a lock with her fingers against her lips. I resigned myself to the fact that Sophia was going to do whatever Sophia wanted. At least this guy wasn't married.

Then Darwin finally arrived. I hardly recognized him. He was easily a full foot taller than he had been the year before, and had acquired a face full of acne. He was dressed the way boys apparently dressed in London: boxy shirt, tapered jeans, and small, square-framed glasses. I hoped there would be a *Star Wars* T-shirt beneath it all, but somehow I knew that was not the case. Still, I was elated to see him and threw my arms around him at the door. He gave me a short squeeze then let go. "Hi, Mir," he said quietly.

"You sound … different," I said. I wanted to make a fuss over him hitting puberty, but realized he was embarrassed.

"I know," he said. "My voice hurts even me to listen to, so I won't be saying much until it's sorted itself out. Now that I'm used to having perfect pitch, this is like the worst thing that could happen to me." He gave a short honk of a laugh and trudged down the hall to where Ma said his room was.

With him in one room and Sophia in another, and Ma in the kitchen, I stood alone in the hallway hearing only the distant whir of an air compressor.

Darwin said he had to practice, so Ma, Sophia, and I left to shop for groceries in Chinatown. The shops were teeming with people, all preparing for the holiday. Ma outlined in detail the dishes she would make for us as we grabbed a cart and dove into the grocery store. My mouth watered as we walked through the rows of noodles: rice, wheat, thick, and thin. Ma's menu seemed endless: lobster smothered with ginger and scallions, steamed sea bass in wine, turnip and taro cakes dotted with dried shrimp, pork dumplings, and fried e-fu noodles in oyster sauce.

While we stood by the tanks full of live fish, Ma announced, "We're having a guest for dinner."

"What? Who?" Sophia demanded. Her prickles went up, and rightly so as the actual big night was always reserved for just family. Ma calmly took the newspaper-wrapped fish from the fish hawker. If there was a man in the picture, I never imagined we would be introduced to him. We did not know how to handle this "mother and her new boyfriend" kind of situation.

"Just a friend from church, a nice man," Ma answered, waving her hand dismissively.

"Man?" Sophia and I asked in unison, and then out of habit, we added, "Jinx!"

"Yes, a church friend," Ma continued as we walked towards the cashier. "His name is William K.C. Koo. He owns the condo."

"So, is this your, like, boyfriend?" Sophia's face soured, while Ma's turned a furious shade of red. She did not answer, handing us food to place on the conveyor belt instead. She was seemingly in a good place, but I didn't want to push just in case there would be another New Year's blowout. I hoped Sophia would behave.

The rest of the day, we pretended there wasn't a William K.C. Koo looming. We all helped Ma cook and adopted a jaunty cheer. Since I had nothing new to report, and Darwin refused to talk, it was up to Sophia to chatter, and chatter she did, filling in cracks and corners with her voice enough for it to become white noise. We settled into a comfortable rhythm, listening to Sophia's tales and following Ma's orders. It was soothing, being her sous-chefs, something we had always enjoyed even when we were very young.

Soon, the condo was filled with the smell of sizzling garlic and onions, and the lighter scent of ginger above that. Surrounded by these smells of home, it was almost easy to forget about my real life, which, frankly, did not smell as nice.

After dinner was prepped, I went to see Darwin in his guest room, painted creamy white just like the rest of the place. "Dar, how's it going?"

He was sitting on one of the beds, fingering some fast lick on a trumpet. "Fine," he said, without looking up. Inside of that one word, his voice pitched high then dove low. Poor kid. I wondered how long it would take to deepen and feel normal to him.

"I got all your letters. The tour sounded really great," I offered.

"Yeah. It was great." He still would not look up at me, his fingers rapidly pushing and releasing the valves on his silver horn. "Why didn't you write back?"

"I did when I could. What do you mean?" I asked.

He finally lifted his head. "You. Didn't. Call. Or. Even. Send. Me. A. Card. For. My. Birthday." He enunciated each word patiently as if I were a lip-reader.

My mind scrambled. Dar's birthday. January 3rd. Oh, shit. How did I let it slip?

"I'm sorry, Darwin. I really am. God, I don't know how I forgot." I felt really bad. I could see it had hurt him. He shrugged and went back to his trumpet.

"Darwin, let me make it up to you, okay? I'll take you out for a celebration dinner tomorrow. You can invite Sophia and Ma if you want. Or just you and me. Anywhere you want," I said, trying to sound enthusiastic.

"Can't. I'm leaving tomorrow morning. Have to get back

to London to play with the symphony. A Royal attendance." Among everything else happening in his voice, I detected a note of sarcasm.

"Oh."

"Forget it," he said. "Don't worry about it."

How was I to tell him that I was worried about it? What was wrong with me? I thought about other birthdays, which now all felt like they were a hundred years ago. Darwin loved Chuck E. Cheese parties and ice cream. Sophia always had to have dounuts. Egg rolls and chicken balls for me, which Ma had called fake Chinese food. Cake and candles. Balloons. Photos. Sophia, Darwin, Ma, Ba, and me. Ba.

"Look, I have to practice," Darwin said, dismissing me.

"But I haven't heard a sound out of your room in three hours!"

He just stared at me with eyes full of anger.

"Oh, okay." I got up and left the room. My stomach felt like poured concrete.

Chapter 18 ⌒

Miu knew that sometimes you had to entertain the enemy at your table. The only thing left was to decide which poison would go best with the roasted pork. Perhaps mask the flavour of arsenic with too much soya sauce?

AT EXACTLY FIVE O'CLOCK the buzzer sounded. Everything was almost ready. Ma whipped off her apron, patted her hair, and rushed out to answer the door. Sophia and I just looked at each other while Darwin joined us in the kitchen and poked at the cooked lobster's eyes. We heard murmurs of a man's voice.

"I guess we should go out there and meet this guy," Sophia hissed.

"The guy she told me about?" Darwin asked.

"Yeah. Ma's got a boyfriend," Sophia answered.

"Why didn't you tell me he was coming?" Darwin whined. Poor Darwin. He winced every time he heard himself speak.

We walked out of the kitchen in single file: eldest first, youngest last. In the living room, a tall man with hair that waved to the left side, stood with Ma who was holding an enormous bundle of yellow lilies. He was dressed in a jacket and tie, and pants that had a crease pressed into them. He also sported a pair of rectangular black-framed glasses. When he saw us, he smiled broadly, revealing straight white teeth. Oh my God, I didn't know whether to laugh or weep. Ma was dating the Chinese Clark Kent.

"Miramar, Sophia, and Darwin, right? It's my pleasure to meet you," he said, with only the slightest hint of a Cantonese accent. He extended his hand to me. I took it and felt his strong grip. He then shook Sophia and Darwin's hands. Sophia smiled curtly, but Darwin kept his face locked onto the carpet.

"Your mother has told me so much about all of you, I feel like I already know you," he beamed. I looked from this stranger to Ma who had a knit in her forehead as she switched the outrageous bouquet from one hand to the other.

Sophia broke the ice. "William K.C. Koo, I presume?" she asked with all the iciness of a princess.

"Sophia, it's Uncle William. Where are your manners?" Ma chided.

"No, Ga Bo, we can be modern here. Call me William," he answered graciously.

"Let's go eat. Come. You must be hungry, and we've been cooking all day," Ma brushed past us and back into the kitchen, leaving the four of us to stand awkwardly together.

We moved to the living room. "Shall we sit?" William asked. He looked at each of us with purpose. "Do you like the condo? You know, I lent it to your Ma. I'm a real estate agent," he said, taking a bunch of business cards out of his leather wallet and giving each of us one. I glanced at the picture of William with his megawatt smile before putting it on the coffee table. "I usually rent it out to Hong Kong businessmen who come for work, but it's been empty. Your mother wanted a change in scenery, so I thought why not? I picked out all the furniture. It's modern, huh?" He seemed to like the word "modern."

We stared back at him blankly. He clapped his hands on his thighs and stood. "I'll go help your mother in the kitchen," he announced. We remained in our seats.

"Well?" Sophia whispered.

I had no words.

"What do you know about this, Dar?" Sophia asked. Darwin shrugged.

"She mentioned one or two times she had a new friend. Some William. But I didn't ask anything. How should I know?" He replied defensively. "You guys know more than I do."

"I don't like him," Sophia said.

"Shhhhh. Stop it. Give the guy a chance. Maybe he's nervous," I answered.

"No, he's too smooth. I don't like him. Isn't it too soon for Ma to date? I mean, shit, I never thought Ma *would* ever date." I knew Sophia had made up her mind. It had never crossed my mind either that Ma would ever find someone else.

Ma did not ask us to help set the table or bring out any of the food and we didn't offer. We came to the table when she called and stared at the huge feast we had prepared. When William announced, "Children, we should say grace," I looked at him like he was an alien. This guy comes into our Ma's house and now was telling us what to do? Who did that? He clasped his hands together and closed his eyes. "Bless us, O Lord, and these your gifts, which we are about to receive from your bounty through Christ our Lord. Amen."

Ma answered clearly, "Amen," while Darwin, Sophia, and I each mumbled something.

Laid out on Ma's new square black dishes, the food that had made me salivate with excitement just moments ago, now looked gelatinous and ugly. Ma kept mounding food into our bowls, while William talked about the real estate market. Apparently things were hot at the moment. Lucrative business. Lots of rich Hong Kong immigrants were snatching up properties in Markham in a rush to get out of Hong Kong before the 1997 China takeover. Only eight years left, he said excitedly. He talked and talked. We listened, half-heartedly, sneaking peeks at him and Ma. Ma's face was held in a tight smile between small mouthfuls of food. The only person who seemed at ease was William K.C. Koo.

Finally, he turned his attention to us. "So, Miramar, what

are you studying at school? Your mother tells me you're at Carleton?"

"Sociology. I was in Journalism, but decided not to major in it," I responded, putting my chopsticks down. I wondered what made me say that.

"And why's that?" William asked while reaching across to pick up a dumpling.

"I don't know. I, uh, just, uh, liked Sociology better, I guess."

"And what are you going to do with it?" he continued, dipping his dumpling in some light soy sauce.

I hadn't been asked about my future in a long time, and I didn't appreciate it coming from Mr. Ultra-Bright Smile Salesman.

"Uh, I don't know, really. After I graduate, I guess I'll look for work," I stammered.

He raised his eyebrows. "Well, get a plan. You need a good plan. Graduate school maybe? Use what you learned. You can even be a real estate agent if you like. Sociology is handy in my trade … you know, you have to be social," he winked as if we were friends.

"Well, maybe. I hadn't thought of it," I said.

He turned to my siblings and opened his arms. "And the two geniuses! I guess I don't have to ask you about your future! You're already making lots of money, huh? Your mother is so proud," he said, smiling and nodding at them.

Sophia and Darwin just sat there, though I could see from Sophia's face that William's flattery had gotten him a point or two. I had to hand it to William K.C. Koo. He had persistence. I sensed he was a master conversationalist, winning over clients easily with his smooth talk. But two lousy points or not, we were going to be harder nuts to crack.

"So, did your mother tell you that we are thinking of travelling to London to pay you a visit this spring, Darwin?" William said, between mouthfuls of taro cake.

Darwin dropped his chopsticks, and they clattered to the ground. Ma jumped out of her seat to fetch him a clean pair.

"Wouldn't that be nice? You must be kind of lonely there, right? We were talking about taking a trip anyway, so why not come visit you?" William dropped this bomb nonchalantly.

"Ma?" Darwin croaked.

"We'll talk later, Darwin. Nothing is planned," Ma said softly, handing him the chopsticks.

"So, what the hell is going on here?" Sophia burst forth, rice flying from her mouth with scattergun effect. Here we go, I thought, resisting the urge to duck under the table.

"I beg your pardon?" William asked, his eyes widening slightly. I hoped he was rattled by Sophia's question. It would prove he was human and not an android.

"Like, are you two dating? Are you boyfriend/girlfriend? What are you?"

"Oh," William demurred, chuckling. "Well, I guess you can say we like each other, a lot." He reached for Ma's hand on the table. Ma flinched ever so slightly. I felt the concrete in my stomach drop to the ground.

"Because I just heard about you today. For the first time. And so, how long has this been going on?" Sophia demanded.

If William detected the irritation in Sophia's voice, he did not show it. "Well, children, I met your mother when I joined the church right after your father's death. Rest his soul," he crossed himself. "We got to know each other through the church events," he paused, adding, "over a long period of time, naturally, since your mother is always flying around the world, checking in on Darwin. But when she was here, we would see each other. She needed some help managing her finances, and the house, so I volunteered."

I had to admire how cool he was. I could not imagine anything Sophia threw at him would faze him.

"Yes, William is a big help to me. To us," Ma said. I knew that was my cue to step in; I could feel the tension starting, burning off my sister like solar flare.

"Thanks for helping, William," I said lamely. "We're just

kind of surprised. But again, I know it's been a lot of work for my mother, so we appreciate your help." I didn't know what to do. Whatever I had just said was not even real. I only didn't want things to escalate.

"You are so welcome, Miramar, children," William grinned.

The rest of dinner was relatively quieter, punctuated by William's compliments to Ma on the tastiness of the food. Sophia had stopped eating. She sat with her arms crossed and glared unflinchingly at William. Darwin ate one tiny grain of rice after another. When Ma finally began to clear the plates, William took them from her and said he would do that chore since she had worked so hard in delivering such a perfect meal for us. He spoke as if on behalf of all of us. Anger roiled in my gut.

After Ma served jasmine tea in the living room, Darwin beat it to his room, while Sophia murmured something about making a phone call. Seconds after she shut her bedroom door, Twisted Sister began blaring, *"we're not gonna take it,"* Sophia's particular battle cry.

Always dependable for my good manners, I stayed with Ma and William in the living room while William sang the praises of condo living. We tried to ignore the screeching music. Soon, I heard another layer of noise emerging from the back. A classical piece, replete with choral singers backed by a full orchestra, was in duel with the metal band.

A few minutes into the din William seemed to get the hint and stood, shaking out his pant legs one after the other to smooth out the creases. "I should get going. I have an early showing tomorrow morning." Ma disappeared into the back rooms to tell Darwin and Sophia to come say goodbye. William couldn't have missed the screaming from both Ma and Sophia through the multiple walls. Both sets of music abruptly stopped, but the condo still reverberated with the terrifying noise. Behind Ma, Sophia and Darwin trudged out of the back rooms.

The unflappable Mr. William K.C. Koo did a sort of bow toward Sophia and something resembling a wave to Darwin. He shook my hand again, and kissed Ma's.

"It has been a wonderful, memorable evening. Thank you for accepting me as a guest at your table," William said grandly. And then, he was gone.

We stood frozen, all four pairs of eyes directed at the door through which he had just passed. Then, all the tension that had been stuffed, bagged, and tied down over the last few hours exploded.

"*What the hell is going on?*" Sophia, as usual, struck the first blow.

"Don't use bad words at me," Ma's voice rose.

"But I want to know what the fuck is going on!"

"What is there to know? William is a good man. He helps me. He helps me! It's not easy for me. After Ba die, I needed help. Okay? Okay?" Ma's voice continued to rise.

"Ma, we just want to know what's going on. Are you serious about him? Just tell us. Please. Calmly," I interjected, trying to redirect us from this road to disaster.

"I don't know. Why do you care? You're all happy. Right? Right?" No one said anything. "So what? You tell me nothing. Why should I tell you? Why?"

Ma had a point. It seemed we did not know anything about each other anymore.

"Maybe I'll marry William. He asked me. Maybe I'll do it. He takes care of many things for me. He's dependable. I need help," Ma continued, her palms held up to the ceiling as if she were asking it for another solution.

Darwin, who had been silent, ran from the room and slammed his door. Sophia took in a great moment of air, then screamed, a piercing scream that shook the glass coffee table. She grabbed the first thing she could find: the glass vase full of flowers and hurled it at the front door where it smashed spectacularly. Water, flowers, and shards of glass splattered everywhere.

"I will never, never accept him. Ma, if you pick him, you lose me," Sophia shrieked before also running to her room and slamming her door.

Ma's face was as pale as the paint on the walls. She looked like a statue. I was also afraid to move, as if any small gesture would cause everything to crumble like dust onto the pristine carpet.

"Ma," I whispered. Ma recoiled as if she had been bitten. She shot off like lightning to her room. Another door slammed. It seemed that this was becoming our new Chinese New Year ritual. Doors slamming, people screaming.

I went to the kitchen and brought back a broom and a garbage bag. Slowly, I picked up the flowers and the million pieces of glass. Some of the shards were large, and others were so tiny they were almost invisible. I hunted for these fragments for a long time, making sure I got them all. After all the evidence was gone, I sat on the couch, staring into space.

Ma said we do not talk of the dead on the New Year, but if ever we needed our Ba it was now. The holiday, his favourite holiday, had become a night when all our pain shot through the family like electricity, severing us even more.

I tried to conjure Ba, but I couldn't remember his voice. Ba was disappearing slowly like an unravelling sweater. I was losing the threads of him. One day soon, there might be nothing left at all. I felt the familiar ache begin to weigh me down again, and I pushed it away hard. I was done with this sadness, sick of it. I got off the couch and paced across the floor, staring down the hall at the closed doors.

"Fine, shut yourselves up in your rooms! Don't talk to me. Don't talk to each other! I don't care anymore!" I screamed into the silence.

I had had enough of this crazy family. It was my turn to scream and hole up in my room. I had enough sense to grab my coat before slamming the front door behind me as hard as I could and getting to the elevator. Downstairs, I stormed by the stupid security guard and his Walkman, straight through that marble lobby, outside the sliding doors and just kept going, out into the city, deep into the frozen, dark night.

It felt good to scream, and great to escape. I was a free agent now. I was an adult. I could come and go. I had *choices*. Who was the chicken shit, now?

Chapter 19 ⌒

Danger lurked around every dark corner in those days. Pui, although blind, knew this more than any of them. The trembling earth told her that horses were coming. It was up to her to scream the battle cry.

I FINALLY RETURNED to the condo around midnight. I had to — my clothes, my wallet, everything was there. Otherwise, I would have walked on forever, disappearing over the edge of this reality and into a new one. When I walked in, the condo was eerily quiet. Meaning, it was quiet with condo sounds. There was that same sad perpetual noise in there I had noticed earlier in the day, the sound of air being released reluctantly, a *phiiiish* with no end. I didn't turn on the lights. The windows had no curtains or blinds, and the lights of the city poured in, spilling onto the blank tableau of the white box.

When I entered the guest room where Sophia and I were to stay, I noticed both beds were still made. Where the hell did that kid go? I pictured her on Bloor Street, at some all-night pizza joint, chatting up a guy about her messed-up family. At this point, I wasn't sure who to feel sorry for: Sophia or the random guy.

I went to Darwin's room to see if he was still up. I had been thinking mainly of him on my wanderings all over the city. If any one of us could get out of this family with a chance of a healthy future, my bet was on Darwin. His door was wide open, and he wasn't there.

That was when the panic hit me between the eyes. I was just starting to get the feeling back into my frozen hands when they began to shake. I ran to Ma's room, the opulent master bedroom, unfurnished but for a king-sized bed that sat low to the ground. It was empty too.

I dashed back to the living room and flicked on all the lights. There was a note on the glass coffee table. "Miramar, Ma had to go to hospital. Toronto Western." The blue ink on the pen had run out by the time Sophia got to "Western" so only an indent of the last word came through. I was stuck to the ground for what seemed like minutes, but it must have only been seconds. Finally, I leaned over and gripped the coffee table hard before running out the door. Later, I wondered if I'd been trying to break it.

At the hospital, I dashed from counter to counter until someone could tell me where I could locate Ma. She was on the eighth floor. The Psychiatric Ward. The Loony Bin. The Cuckoo's Nest. I rode the elevator up to the eighth, trying to drown my thoughts in the Muzak version of "You've Got a Friend." When the doors opened, I could already see Sophia and Darwin far down the hall, sitting on benches against the walls of the corridor. They stared right at me.

I ran to them as quickly as I could, even though I wanted to run the other way, back into the elevator, back into the cab that took me here, back to the moment when I first walked into Ma's condo earlier that morning. I did not know what I would have done differently, but I would have found a million things I could have changed. Anything to take this back.

Sophia and Darwin remained seated. Sophia's eyes were red and swollen. Darwin had blue shadows like bruises beneath his. Deep red scratches ran down one of his cheeks, claiming bloodied pimples along the way. Before I even had to ask, Sophia said in a small voice, "Ma had one of her episodes. I heard her screaming. It was about the hands again. I went in to see her, and she didn't even recognize me. She thought I was going to kill her or something. Then Darwin came in, and she went at him like he was trying to attack her. We were calling for you, but you weren't there." She started to scratch at the sleeves of her sweater.

"I went out. Didn't you hear me?" I asked. How could they not have heard my dramatic exit?

Sophia glared at me. "No. I thought you were in the living room the whole time."

"I had my headphones on. I didn't hear you go out," Darwin said flatly.

Here I had thought I had finally drawn a line in the sand, and they had not even noticed. I felt guilty as hell. They'd needed me, and I had not been there. Instead, I was skulking through the city like some rebellious kid having a temper tantrum. Sitting on the bench, all small and huddled, they looked like the scared children I used to remember as my real brother and sister. When she was little, Sophia used to be afraid of thunder and would scramble up to my bed any time there was a storm. And Darwin looked like the time he wet his pants in Grade 1, and I had to pick him up from the school office to take him home.

"Are you all right, Dar?" I asked him. I ran my finger lightly over his injured face. He nodded, but tears dripped down his cheeks. I sank onto the bench and hugged him to me. He was my little brother again. "Sophia, come here," I ordered. She stood from her seat on the bench and came around to sit beside me. I held her hand and she gripped mine hard.

"Is she going to be okay?" I asked her.

"I don't know. The doctor wanted to talk to you because you're the only one of age in the family. They said she was stable. Whatever that means."

"Okay, you two. Stay here. I'll be right back." I pulled Sophia close to Darwin so she could hold him.

I went to the reception desk, and they said I could see Ma.

This surprised me. All those times Ba had taken her to the hospital, it had never come up that we would be allowed to see her, and here they said I could go in easily as if she were recovering from a paper cut. All those times he had taken her away, and we had never even asked if we could visit.

I felt rotten and my stomach quivered; I had no idea what to expect. Ba had always made it sound like Ma was in a posh hotel getting room service, while I let my cinematic mind run away with the image of her room as a padded cell, her arms twisted in a straightjacket, and electrodes attached to her head.

As I pushed open her room door, I steeled myself for any variation of these themes. But inside this very normal hospital room, lay Ma in a normal bed. It was clean, not scary, and smelled of disinfectant and something else I could not place that reminded me of mushrooms, dampness, rain.

I stood at the rail of the bed and looked down at her face. She had seemed so young a few hours earlier and now, her skin was slack and pulled at her cheekbones. Her mouth was slightly open, and a trickle of saliva was sliding down her chin. Her hair at the roots was white. I stared at the place where her black hair, which I had always thought was natural, and her real hair met. I marvelled that out of everything that had happened, all the new information and pain, the fact that Ma coloured her hair was what was catching me most off guard.

After a moment, the doctor appeared beside me, startling me out of my thoughts. She was Chinese. I had pictured an elderly white man, maybe someone who looked like Sigmund Freud. She was young too, probably fresh out of school. I bet her parents were proud. "You must be Miramar."

"Yes, I am."

"I'm Dr. Pang. I have located your mother's files from Scarborough General. It seems she suffers from episodes of panic attacks and depression. The hallucinations may be related to some kind of trauma. I assume you know this?"

I shook my head. The shapeless thing that Ma suffered from

now had names. "Well, her chart says she had been on tricyclics on and off again for almost nine years. These are not aspirins, but very serious medications that have accumulative properties and need to be taken regularly as a course of treatment, not as a stop-gap solution."

I nodded again. I did not really know what to make of all of this information, but the doctor was talking to me like I was the one responsible. I watched the words come out of the doctor's mouth like accusations. Did she think I was stupid for not knowing any of this? I felt stupid.

"We've got her sedated, so she'll sleep for some time. I recommend that we keep her here at least for a few days to come up with another avenue of treatment." Dr. Pang looked at me and waited. I looked at Ma. I didn't know what I was supposed to say. "Is that okay, Miramar?" she asked.

"Oh, yes. If that's what you think…" I answered.

The doctor nodded and then proceeded to walk out.

"Thank you," I called after her.

I went into the hall to tell Sophia and Darwin what the doctor had said. I was surprised to see William K.C. Koo standing with them. I slowed down my steps, but he turned.

"Miramar. How is she?" He strode toward me.

"She's all right," I answered, my eyes focused on Sophia and Darwin behind him.

"I had to call him, Mir. I didn't know what else to do," Sophia said.

"She's all right. She has to stay for a few days, but she's sleeping now," I said.

I went back to the bench to join my sister and brother. "I'll stay here with her. I know you guys have to leave tomorrow." As soon as I said it, I felt a cold wind rush through my chest. I didn't want them to go, to leave me alone. This was Ba's job, not mine. I looked at them. "Why don't you just stay a few more days? No one would fault you for that."

Darwin looked like a drenched puppy. "No, I think I'm

gonna go. I mean, if she's okay and all," Darwin mumbled toward his feet. Sophia said she would stay an extra day, but that she needed to be back to give an important lecture. So much for swearing that we would come together for Chinese New Year. They were both bailing when it was most important for them to stay.

I felt so heavy but tried to smile. "Sure, of course. And you know Ma. She'll be back to normal in no time. A week tops." I tried to sound light. "Anything I can do, just count on it!" William said. I looked up at his neat face and tidy hair and wanted to slap him. She was my mother; he had no place here. I wanted to blame him for all of this. William was nothing, an unwelcome stranger to our family. Darwin would go, Sophia would go too, and I would be alone with him. I looked at the puke-green walls, seething.

Chapter 20 ⟿

Hei was a goddess from the Eight Immortals. They were the ultimate champions of the world, criss-crossing China in a bid to end oppression to humankind. Together, the eight siblings were invincible, but one day, Hei lost her companions and was forced to face the Dragon Lord on her own when she tried to save a pack of dogs trapped in a cave. The Dragon Lord told her it was impossible since he had intended to raise them to be the dogs of hell, the guardians of the underworld. Without the other warriors, she was no match for the Dragon Lord who whipped her around with his tail covered in emerald scales. She leapt from bamboo branch to branch, finally losing her balance and falling into a cluster of clouds. Hei fell without end, howling from defeat and sadness.

THE NEXT AFTERNOON Darwin returned to London, as silent and sullen as he had arrived. The long scratches on his face were worse in the morning, branding him like angry claw marks. I took his bag to the airport limo for him, expecting a hug or a kiss. Instead, he slid himself into the leather seat before I could say goodbye. He waved without looking up and shut the door.

Sophia and I sat with Ma in silence while she slept most of the whole day. They must have really knocked her out. Sophia needed to do some work for Professor Gorky's lecture on larger polygons, so in the hours we had before her evening train back to Montreal, I asked her to explain it to me, anything to make conversation. She sighed as if I were a child asking for the meaning of life. I let it go. This was not a time to get mad at Sophia, however tempting it was. I was just glad she wasn't tearing at her arms again. On the second day, I was alone with Ma. I wanted her to wake up, but at the same time, I was glad she was taking her sweet time because I would not have known what to say to her.

I spent most of my time staring out the window at the parking lot below, watching people like ants get in and out of snow-speckled cars, and thought about my walk from a few nights before. It had been about zero degrees, lightly windy, and clear like a brand new window. All the lights on University Avenue had flickered like stars in the dark. While I walked, I had allowed myself to sink into memory: our last Chinese New Year with Ba. Ma had been sick with the flu, so the three of us kids and Ba had tried to cook New Year's dinner. It had been a disaster. We had overcooked the noodles into a sticky mush; the chicken's skin had crisped up golden, making us proud, but cutting into it was another story: the flesh was pink and raw. Ba had tried to wash the crabs, but they scrabbled around the kitchen sink trying to crawl out. Darwin had run into his room for his Jedi robes and returned, waving his light saber at them like they were Stormtroopers.

We had been so busy squealing about the crabs, that Ma had finally shuffled out of her bedroom looking like the walking dead, took one look at us, and screamed for all of us to stop. We, in turn, had looked at each other and howled with laughter. Even Ma had cracked a smile. Ba finally ordered takeout pizza while Ma put the crabs out of their misery in the wok, then returned to bed. Our dinner was a party-sized pepperoni pizza and fresh-water crab, and we ate it up like it was a feast for kings.

Thinking about this had made my sinuses feel itchy and full like I was holding in a sneeze, so I had walked faster, continuing to criss-cross the city streets, pausing to stare at the high-rises and catching glimpses of seagulls arcing through the air in search of food on the ground. Eventually, I found myself in Chinatown. It was late and most of the stores had closed. The only people out were nicely dressed families descending from restaurants where they had probably had their New Year's dinners. The usual storefront lights were still on and the day's garbage was bundled on the curb, but devoid of the usual hustle and bustle that one could mistake for happiness, for life being lived fully, and the streets felt unsafe and gloomy.

I walked by the Golden Harvest Theatre, the cinema where Ba and I had spent so many Sunday afternoons. A man was sitting on the steps, smoke trailing lazily up from a cigarette he had in his ungloved hands. I wondered, as I widened my berth to walk by, whether he was cold, maybe homeless.

"Yo. Got a cigarette, *lang lui*?" *Lang lui,* pretty girl. That was the last thing I felt like.

"Nope. Sorry," I answered, quickening my steps.

"Ya want one?" He held his cigarette up toward me.

I could not help it. I laughed out loud and looked at him. It had not been a normal night, and my loneliness wanted the romance of smoke wafting up from my fingers. Suddenly, I had wanted nothing more than to be the kind of person who talked to strangers and accepted their cigarettes. To be that free.

I backed up, approached him, and saw a young face. He could have even been my age, and was kind of cute. His eyes drooped down toward the corners like moons as he smiled. He had a long face with slender lips, the mouth of a woman.

"I'm Mouse," he said as he offered his open pack of cigarettes. I slid a cigarette out along with a lighter. I lit the cigarette, inhaling deeply to draw in the fire. It made me cough, and soon I was doubled-up, hacking into my hands. Mouse stood and patted my back the way my parents used to when I had choked on something.

"Thanks," I said, straightening up, embarrassed. I handed

him back his cigarette and started to walk away, feeling ridiculous talking to a stranger, letting him touch me, and then looking like an idiot.

"You're welcome!" he called after me.

The cigarette had given me a headache. I wondered how I was ever able to match Jerry smoke for smoke when we were together. I had done a lot of weird things to fit in with Jerry and the North Bay crowd. But, of course, I never quite fit in, and that was easy for me to see now. Still, being dumped smarted, like the aftermath of a slap.

I wondered what Jerry was doing that very moment that I found myself walking north on Spadina Avenue. Was he having sex with the old/new girlfriend? Was he biting the nape of her neck the way he used to bite mine? Such thoughts made me feel sick and heavy but I could not stop them rushing at me. I wanted to go home, but that home sat empty in Scarborough. I had no idea if the lights still worked. Whether it had heat. Numb from the cold, I headed back to the only place I had left to go, Ma's condo.

The next afternoon, William came by to see Ma. He had told the nurses that he was Ma's fiancé. It could have been true for all I knew, and I felt outraged and helpless. He sat on the other side of her and held her hand. I hated that he didn't mind sitting there, holding my mother's hand, right in front of me, invading my space, my time with her. He did things he should have done in private: whisper in her ear, caress her hand. I didn't get it; Ma used to bat Ba away whenever he tried to be affectionate. Any show of love made her jump like she had touched a snake. "*Aiya, Mm ho la!*" Enough! she used to screech. I wanted to whip William's hand away and shout too. But instead I sat there, stupid, like I was the third wheel in my own life.

"Miramar, what happened?" he asked, looking up at me. "I don't understand."

I thought of the million answers I could give him. What happened? Search me, pal. "Ma has ... a condition. I don't know if she ever talked about it," I began. He shook his head. "Maybe you can ask her when she's better," I said. This was the only answer I would give to William K.C. Koo. He was not my family, and Ma would have to decide whether he was hers.

Ma woke up later that afternoon. William had long gone back to work. I had a paper due and an exam the following week, but I was reading an old *People* magazine I had stolen out of the waiting room. School seemed like another world, another lifetime. Besides, this was the *25 Most Intriguing People of 1987* issue. An education in its own right, I reasoned.

I was deep in an article about Cher when Ma's eyes fluttered open. "Miramar?"

"Ma?" I dropped the magazine.

"Where am I? What's happening?" She rubbed her head. "Wah. Such a headache." I saw her eyes travel over the sterile room, the light blue sheets covering her body, the IV hooked into her arm, but she looked confused like nothing was registering.

"You're okay, Ma. We're in the hospital. You just had a big sleep."

"It happened again," she turned her head away and sighed. She was silent for a long time, staring at the wall. "You know Ba was the one who wanted to come to Canada," she said so quietly I barely heard her. "He was the one who said it would be a good life for all of you. A big house. A yard. You would all grow up healthy and smart." I pulled my chair closer, so I would not miss a word.

"He went on and on. For years. You were just born when he started. Then Sophia. Finally, I said, okay. Why not? He knew best." She sighed again.

"He was always crazy for English. Wanted to speak to you both in English right away so you would learn. *Ka-La-Dai.*

Always going on about *Ka-La-Dai*. Open spaces, good air, lots of opportunities there, he said. So, we came." I had never heard my Ma talk like this before. She never referred to the past, back in Hong Kong. I used to beg her to tell me stories of when we were there, but she would never do it.

"We came in February. Darwin was still in my arms. We stepped outside of the airport, and I screamed from the cold. *Aiya!* It was a terrifying cold. I hugged all of you to me, so you didn't freeze," she grimaced. "Your Ba convinced me he loved it. He loved everything about *Ka-La-Dai*. We used to live in that dirty apartment, remember? No, you were too young to remember. The pigeons used to make nests on the balcony. So filthy. Poo everywhere. Ba convinced me he loved the pigeons too. Everyone should have a home, he said. He even took some of the eggs out of the nest and tried to hatch them in the oven for you girls. Your crazy Ba."

I did not remember any of this, but could very well see my Ba doing this.

"And look what happened? I became the one who went *chi seen*. Crazy! Funny, ha?" She turned to me then. "I hated it here. I hated everything. I hated the snow, I hated the heat, I hated the people, I hated the house, I hated the sky. I went — what do you say in English — 'cuckoo'!" She spat the words out.

"I wanted to go home. Back to my friends. Back to where people didn't look at me like I was an animal. I wanted my old neighbourhood. I wanted to smell the harbour." She was really scaring me, but I could not tear my eyes from her face, all twisted now in raw pain.

She was not trying to control her tears; they fell and fell. Her nose ran. I bent over and held her. I had never embraced my mother before, and she felt fragile as if I could break her if I hugged her too hard. She did not hug me back. Her arms stayed limp on the bed.

"I couldn't ask Ba to leave. You were all happy here. He was right. You three children growing up, big and strong. Smart.

Going to school. It was right to come. Ba was right. But then, why couldn't I be happy?"

"I don't know, Ma. I'm sorry. I didn't know," I murmured. I finally let her go. She sank back into the pillow and closed her eyes. I sat back down and kicked at the magazine on the floor.

She didn't say any more to me that day. Later that night, I phoned Sophia and Darwin to tell them that she had woken up, and had even eaten a little.

There was relief in Sophia's voice. "It was my fault, wasn't it?" She sounded so tiny.

"Oh, Sophia," I exhaled loudly. I wasn't in the mood to console my sister. I was exhausted. Would it have hurt her to ask how I was? "It wasn't your fault. Ma's been like this for a while, you know."

"But I know I piss her off. I just get so mad her. Sometimes, I feel like she just doesn't like me. And then we fight..." she paused. "Maybe I should have been nicer to William."

"Sophia, you can tell her this yourself. As for not liking you, you don't seriously believe that. You're her daughter. She loves you. You may even be her favourite."

"Tell her? Mir, I can hardly carry on a conversation with her half the time these days. All of our phone calls end up with one of us hanging up. Everything I do is wrong. If I really told her what's going on with me, she would flip. Maybe get way worse than she already is."

"Well, you can't blame yourself. Ma's problems are ... chemical. That's what the doctor said. Just try to be easier on her. She's had a rough time. She's the only parent we've got," I said this last sentence as an afterthought. Once said, the gravity of it weighed on me.

I thought about telling her what Ma had told me, but knew Sophia didn't have the fortitude to handle such a burden. I thought about the scratches on her arms and wondered if she was doing it even now on the phone with me. For all her tough act, I knew that when it came to Ma, Sophia was just a little girl who needed to be reassured that everything was going to be all right. I wished I could do that for her now, the way Ba had done it for all of us.

While I was sure Darwin was relieved too, he was back to his one-word sentences.

"How's your face?" I asked.

"Good."

"Healing okay?"

"Yup."

Okay, then. One mother in the pysch ward, heavily sedated, check. One sister blaming herself for her mother's psychotic episode, check. One brother who preferred to grunt monosyllabic words rather than have a real conversation about any of this, check. One father dead, check. Family falling into pieces before my eyes, check. I wondered where that left me.

It was serious what Ma had said, and I did not have the energy to think about it. It meant that during our whole lives together, she had been trying to be happy, but failing, and lying to us all.

When I arrived at the hospital in the morning, William was already there. Ma was sitting up in bed, dressed in a jogging suit. She smiled widely at me when I entered. Dr. Pang was also there, all business with her lab coat and files. Confused, I looked from Ma to William to Dr. Pang, wondering why I felt like I was interrupting something.

"There you are!" William announced like I was the guest.

"*Nui, nui*. I can go home!" Ma pronounced this like she had won a trip to Hawaii.

"Yes, she can. Make sure she is good with taking her medication and coming in for her appointments so I can monitor how it's working," Dr. Pang spoke to me like Ma was my kid.

"Oh, don't worry, Doctor. I will be making sure she does everything she is supposed to," William replied. Who was talking to him? Dr. Pang acquiesced to William and for the first time, I saw her smile. I guess William did have some people skills, or Dr. Pang finally found someone she felt she could trust with Ma's care. I believed the latter. Could not blame her, really. Every time she talked to me about Ma's condition, I just stared at her with my mouth open.

She bent down to Ma and said, "Be good." Ma gave Dr. Pang her best Catholic smile.

"Miramar, I have it all taken care of. Your Ma will be staying with me at my house until she feels better. You don't have to worry about a thing. Go back to Ottawa to your classes. We'll be in touch to tell you how she is," William stated. Ma gave him the same congenial smile.

"Ma," I began. Her serene smile was still there. "Is that okay with you?"

"Yes, yes. All okay," she said softly. William was holding her hand again, and she was letting him. They were staring at each other, and it seemed right for me to leave.

I wanted to slap William's smug face and Ma's sedative-laced grin, but instead, I walked away. I crossed the long hallway full of fluorescent lights. They were so bright, they burned into me. I was sweating under my scarf. I pressed the elevator button, once and then I banged it over and over. When the elevator finally came, I stepped in and leaned against the wall. I went back to the condo, packed my bags, and caught the first bus to Ottawa. Ma had chosen. What could I offer her? Would I leave school and move into her condo? Would I be able to talk her back from her ledges? Yes. I would have done all of these things and more if she had given me the opportunity. But perhaps William could give her what none of us could, not me, not Sophia, nor Darwin, not even Ba.

The thought of Ba felt like a stab in my heart. Did Ma think so little of his memory that she was ready to fly into William's arms? Ba had given everything to us, even his life just so he could get home to us a little earlier. I could accept

Ma betraying me or even Darwin and Sophia, but I couldn't accept this betrayal to Ba.

What Ma had told me played over and over in my head. The Ma I knew who could not stop being useful to everyone, the Ma who played *mah jong* passionately with her friends, the Ma my Ba adored. All of it was false. She had been unhappy the whole time, having us believe that she loved us. Meanwhile, she lived her life with a million regrets. She regretted everything, and the only way out, the only way to escape us, was to go nuts. She thought we were so awful? Then, to the hell with her.

I knew then what was between the nuthouse and the grave — nowhere. I was nowhere.

Chapter 21 ⇌

Crawling to the edge of the lake, Wai-ling was desperately thirsty. Her armour was in pieces, and she bled from where the arrow was stuck in her leg. Under the night sky, she scooped water into her mouth frantically, crying as she drank. After, she yanked the arrow from her limb and laid on her back. She would either die here or be born anew. Either way, she was conspiring with the stars.

WHEN I GOT BACK to Ottawa, I sorted through my things. I couldn't be with Ma, but I realized on the bus that I couldn't be in Ottawa anymore either. I found a few photos of Jerry tucked into a mostly unused journal. There were no photos of us together. It felt so long enough ago that I could almost believe it never happened. I threw the pictures away, wondering if we had ever existed as a couple at all. I wasn't angry with Jerry anymore, just numb.

I gathered the "Dormant" client files and shoved them in my suitcase then poured my *kung fu* videos on top. My makeup, including Revlon's "Spring Blush," went into the garbage bag. It took me less than fifteen minutes to pack all my worldly belongings into the same suitcases I had brought to Ottawa. By the time I was finished, I had less than I had originally brought with me a year and a half ago when I moved there.

I went to the bank and closed my account. I had over five thousand dollars. I asked the teller for an envelope and stuck it into my jacket pocket. I thought about phoning Kathleen to say goodbye. She had been nice to me. She had tried, in her own way, to watch out for me. I wanted to thank her, but I couldn't decide how to begin. Maybe I would write her a letter, one day, when I could actually tell her something worth saying.

I boarded another Greyhound. This time, I was heading back in the direction whence I came. This time, however, instead of being a young, promising university student, I was going back as a slightly older, hardly wiser, university drop-out.

Chapter 22 〜

Lai Wing had to hide from her family who was forcing her into an arranged marriage she did not want. Her would-be groom was an old, ugly, rich guy with a hairy mole on his chin. Lai Wing had to find a way to carve out her own life, cut loose from family and funds. What her parents, her shunned groom, or anyone from the village did not account for was her industriousness, tenacity and deadly kung fu prowess. With a ninja-like cloak, she became a hired assassin, avenging people for extortion from greedy landlords. Lai Wing was revered at the end of it all. (In the background: Aretha Franklin singing "R-E-S-P-E-C-T.")

BACK IN TORONTO, I checked into a cheap hotel on King Street and started to look at apartments for rent. I saw a bunch, including a flat in an old rambling house in Chinatown. It had peeling red paint on the brick, and it leaned slightly to the left. It stood side by side other houses that also looked to be in various stages of dilapidation. An ancient Italian woman lived downstairs and was officially my landlord although it was her son who rented the upstairs apartment to me.

"She don't speak English." He had waved in his mother's direction dismissively when he gave me the tour.

Downstairs, I looked in the direction of the open front door and saw the wizened woman sitting in a chair in the darkened hallway. She peeked out, her head extending on her neck like a turtle's, and followed me with her eyes.

As I toured the apartment, the son gave me the story of the

house. He had grown up there. His parents had emigrated from Italy in the 1940s. His dad was a construction worker. I was charmed by the place. The ceilings were more than ten feet high. The living room had two large windows that almost spanned the entire wall and looked out into the street. This room would make a good *kung fu* space.

There was a large kitchen, big enough for a table, an even larger bedroom that walked out onto a fire escape, and a tiny bathroom with a shower stall. Different layers of wallpaper showed through various tears, but the rooms were filled with light. When I opened all the windows, the most delicious cross-wind moved through the house. I didn't need to think. "I'll take it," I said, and began pulling hundreds out of my wallet.

The man paused, looked at me, and laughed, a hearty, warm laugh. "I like it when a woman knows what she likes," he said, then smiled. "It's a happy house. You'll see."

He left me alone to enjoy my new home for a minute. As I walked through my empty apartment, I was surprised by an excitement that came over me. A year and a half ago, I was a suburban teenager thrilled about launching my adult life — university, employment, and maybe, deep in the future, marriage and a family of my own. All those markers stretched ahead of me, a map with clearly marked signs and signals. Was life so random that one careless move while crossing the road could change the course of everything? Could one second shift the history of the world and everything in it? I only knew that this empty apartment, this moment, this Miramar was not supposed to be part of the trip. While it didn't feel like a step backwards, it was definitely a step outside. No more maps; I was on a detour.

In the next week, I gathered furniture from the local Salvation Army and got creative with milk crates that I pilfered from the corner store, assembling and reassembling the boxes into various pieces of furniture: a coffee table, a bookshelf, a stool, a headboard and frame for my futon. An old floor lamp fringed in long cracked glass beads that someone had discarded on the sidewalk cast a warm tangerine glow at night. In the giant discount store Honest Ed's, I picked up a pot, some utensils, and a wok. Every time I went in or out, the old lady watched me from her chair in the hallway. I always shouted a cheery, "Hello." She ignored me the entire first week, and then, she started to nod in acknowledgement. One day, she started to wave back.

In the mornings, I developed a routine: I would walk to the corner store and a fat ginger cat would greet me with a drawn-out *meow*. I would reach down and pet her as she languidly brushed against my leg. I would buy a newspaper then walk to Kim Moon Bakery and select a *dan tat*, a pastry and egg custard still warm from the oven. Back at my apartment, I would sit in my kitchen and nibble the egg tart while flipping through the classified ads. I still had a wad of cash rolled up under my futon mattress, but I knew that would not last forever. I needed to find work because I was determined not to phone the lawyer and redirect my monthly allowance from Ba's estate and Sophia and Darwin's earnings to another bank account. There were cashier positions in donut shops and data entry clerks in office buildings. I sent out my meagre résumé to all of them. The rest of the day, I watched my *kung fu* films and soap operas while I waited for the phone to ring. It never did. All I had to claim was a high-school education and one not too illustrious year of university. Besides my short stint at the Counselling Centre as receptionist, I had no work experience. Nada. Zilch. Nothing.

Finally, as spring approached, I got a call back. It was for a job as receptionist at a community centre in Toronto's east end. I went to the Salvation Army and bought a black blazer and skirt for the interview. The blazer had a hint of shoulder pad, and it actually looked nice on me. I pulled my wayward hair into a tight ponytail off my face and stuck my legs into a pair of black pantyhose. My weight had been on a rollercoaster in the last couple of years, but now, it was just between my "rocky road ice cream" phase and my "Jerry-obsessed skinny era."

When I got to the community centre, I got nervous. As soon as I walked in, I was met with a sour smell. In the lounge area, a cluster of what appeared to be homeless people sat around a TV. Smoke rose from a giant ashtray in the middle of the table.

At last, I was called into the interview and sat across from a panel of judges, or should I say, my possible employers. There were three of them. My near hermit-like existence did not prepare me for the questions that came like quick-fire from these strangers. I stuttered. I made incomplete sentences. I uttered too many "uhhhs" and "ummms." My vision was beginning to blur from the effort of speaking.

"What would you do if someone came to the centre who was intoxicated and disruptive?" the woman in gold-rimmed glasses asked.

"Um," I began, trying to think quickly, "I would ask the person politely to leave. Then, maybe I should call the police?"

"Well, we do have crisis counsellors on staff," a man in a sports shirt replied. He seemed to be the most laid-back of the group. He had a ponytail and smiled a lot.

"Oh, okay. In that case, I would call the crisis counsellor to deal with the situation," I answered. Was this a trick question? They all nodded at me, writing in their notepads.

"Miramar, do you speak Cantonese?" the woman in the pink sweater asked as if it had just occurred to her that this was important information.

"Yeeees," I answered tentatively. In truth, I spoke Cantonese like a child, my tongue frozen upon immigration.

"Oh!" Everyone's demeanour suddenly became warm. Gold-Rimmed Woman looked at Man In Sports Shirt who looked over at Woman In Pink. There were more nods and smiles. Then, "We know you didn't apply for this position, but would you be interested in being a settlement counsellor?"

I had no idea what a "settlement counsellor "was, but it sounded like it paid more than a receptionist so I nodded. This seemed to make them happy.

My job was to do intake. I interviewed the new immigrants when they filed in about their needs and then found the right service to send them to. The interview was standard. I was given a sheet with questions to ask, information to take down, and a progress report to follow up on in six months. All this data was then filed with the federal government so they had a record that newcomers were being fully "integrated" into their new circumstances. Since a large number of them were Chinese, the centre needed someone who could translate this information into the prescribed boxes on the government forms.

William was right; the Chinese from Hong Kong were streaming into Canada, fearful of what the 1997 change of sovereignty to China would bring. Once upon a time, our family had to go to Chinatown to see groups of Chinese people, and now they (or we) seemed to be everywhere.

They needed assistance with housing (how did you find an affordable place to settle three generations of a family?); finances (what were you to do when you discovered that despite being a professional, you could not get a job because your qualifications did not actually count for squat in Canada?); domestic violence (where were you to go to be safe when your husband was beating the crap out of you and you spoke no English?); schooling (what were you to do when your kid is being called a "chink" every single day at school and the administration refused to do anything?), and on and on. It was exhausting and exhilarating at the same time. My job was to move these people and their complaints forward. Each problem to its proper channel. After only a month, I knew many of these channels led to dead ends or to an endless loop of more bureaucratic channels.

My clients looked at me with desperate faces as if I held the map to this strange, new place. Sometimes, I did. Sometimes, the sun and stars aligned and shined on the path to the solution. People got housed, employed, and enrolled in English classes. These moments made me feel useful, like my life had purpose. Other times, the futility of the job made my blood boil. Innocent people were being taken advantage of, were paid below minimum wage, were fired and rehired at the whim of factory owners, and were charged ridiculous rent to live in slums. Then I felt impotent and could only vent my frustrations through *kung fu* fantasies at home.

I was continually grateful I had had the prescience to take an apartment with such an enormous living room. At night, after I got home and changed into my sweats, I fought imagined government officials who denied people their rights. A whole village of immigrants was relying on me to topple the government and free them from their troubles. I stormed into the Parliament Buildings, threw open the doors of the House of Commons, and unleashed my furious fists at the MPs. The people (a generic people at this point made up of all colours, ages, and sizes) followed me in, and reclaimed the country as their own. If the old woman downstairs ever wondered what the commotion was overhead, she never let on.

The trouble with living alone, I began to notice, was that there was no one to temper me, to help me keep my fantasy life and real life distinct. I grew bolder at work, pushing people to answer my questions while my clients sat across from me, fatigue lining their faces. One couple had gotten their heat turned off in their apartment because, according to the calendar, it was spring. Yet the weather couldn't read that even in April it was still cold and that, sometimes, there were still sudden snow flurries. The couple (he was a sheet worker and she was pregnant), were terrified of being kicked out of their apartment if they complained.

"I don't mind for myself. But my wife. She's pregnant. She's not used to the cold," he told me in his rapid Cantonese.

I called the legal clinic down the street. They told me that the couple had to first come in and qualify for legal aid and then make a complaint with the Landlord and Tenant Board, and on and on and on it went. It would be July by the time anything happened.

"What's your landlord's number?" I asked him in my halting Cantonese. He handed me a worn piece of paper. The landlord's name was also Chinese. This made me furious. Why would he do that to his own people? I dialled the number.

"*Wai? Wai?*" a man answered in Cantonese.

"Hello, may I speak to Mr. Chow?" I asked in a clipped, professional voice. I decided to talk in English. My home advantage.

"Ah, yes, that's me," he answered, his voice heavily accented.

"I am calling from the city. I have been notified that you do not have heat on in the building at 456 Huron Street. This is your property, is it not?"

"Yes, yes!"

"We have become aware that you have shut off heat to that building, violating Toronto Municipal Code Article 497.2. Are you aware of this, Mr. Chow?"

"No, no violations. No!" he stammered.

"I understand that you would not want to be fined for this. Since this is your first violation, I won't penalize you. But you must turn on the heat until the temperature outside reaches eighteen degrees Celsius. Am I clear?"

"Yes, yes, sorry. Sorry, madam." I could practically hear him sweating.

"Good, Mr. Chow. My agents will be coming by to check on the property from time to time to make sure you are operating under the legal terms. Have a good day," I said and hung up.

The couple looked at me, their faces crinkled up with questions.

"It's okay now. You'll have heat," I told them in Cantonese. Relief swept through their faces. They stood up and both of them clasped my hands. "Thank you, thank you," they said, bowing. The young woman reached into her large handbag and pressed a large cold globe into my hand. I looked down; it was an orange, almost neon in colour with a large navel at its tip. I was touched. It was as if she had given me a pound of gold.

I could not believe what I'd done. It was my first taste of victory in my life. I could not wait to do it again.

Chapter 23 ~

The Monkey King can be charming. But he has no loyalties to anyone but himself. Take care. He is capable of wreaking havoc in both heaven and earth. Or, at the very least, he could just be a player.

ONE NIGHT IN JUNE, I was on my way home from work on the streetcar, my stomach growling loudly. I bent this way and that in my seat, hoping to suffocate the sounds with the rolls of fat around my waist. I thought about the packet of instant ramen on my kitchen shelf that I would make as soon as I got home.

Ramen was as basic as it came, so I let my imagination adorn it with slivers of green onion, balls of fried tofu, and baby bok choy, until I was jostled out of my noodle daydream by the boom of a baritone voice, "Hallo, hallo! We'come, we'come." I craned my neck between the people to see who was speaking, and recognized him right away. It was the guy who had given me a cigarette the night Ma was hospitalized. He had hopped onto the car and was personally escorting passengers off. It would have been hilarious and cute and completely ridiculous if it had been anyone else, but I did not want to see him or him to see me. He jumped onto the pavement, swivelled around on one foot, and turned to the westbound traffic with sweeping arms as if he were conducting a grand orchestra and the cars were his musicians. Around his arms, dozens of bright strips of fabric flew in all directions, giving him the mesmerizing effect of a maypole.

The streetcar pulled away, and I stayed on. The scene had rattled something in me, and it was worth the extra walk. A murmur ran through the car afterward; some of the passengers were puzzled, some were alarmed, some laughed, and others pretended not to notice. I wondered how many of them tagged him as "a crazy Chinaman."

Shortly after that, I saw Mouse again, this time at the laundromat near my apartment. He was leaning against the wall, humming along to something on his Walkman when I approached with my wicker basket full of dirty clothes. His hair was different —the sides closely shaved with long strands in the middle falling to the left and right like a fake mohawk. His face was unlined, his skin smooth and tanned. He could have been anywhere from sixteen to twenty-five.

He nodded in time and finished his cigarette with a long drag before flicking it onto the road. He turned around and looked straight at me. I quickened my steps into the laundromat. He followed me in and yelled, "Hello," as if we were long-lost friends.

"*Lang lui*, how are you?"

I turned to face him, my basket in front of my chest. He laughed at me. "Remember? I gave you a cigarette once." He smiled at me. He didn't look deranged. The light was streaming through the windows, and I got a good look at his face. He was cute. Maybe he was crazy, but he was definitely cute. His eyes were kind; the colour of milk chocolate. And there was that shapely mouth again, the middle of the top lip forming a perfect heart. He was wearing a Malcolm X T-shirt and jeans and was about half a foot taller than me. Thankfully, his ribbons were nowhere to be seen.

"Oh, yeah. I remember." I felt bad for pretending to forget. I put my basket on a machine and started to load.

"So, how are you, *lang lui*?" He leaned against the next machine. I had nowhere to escape to.

"I'm okay. You?" I fumbled in my pockets for quarters.

"Here, let me." He inserted two quarters into the slots.

"Oh, you don't have to do that," I protested.

"Done." He pushed the slot back and the quarters disappeared.

"Okay. Thanks."

"*Lang lui*, you wanna smoke?"

"No, thanks. I don't really smoke," I said.

"Want a coffee?" he offered.

"Do you have laundry here? Or are you just hanging out?" Maybe I was being impolite, but the memory of him at the intersection made me nervous to be so close to him.

"I'm just waiting around for a *lang lui* to come along so I can eat her for lunch," he replied with a straight face.

I looked at him wide-eyed.

Then he laughed, a full belly wallop of a laugh and slapped the top of a machine. "I'm doing my laundry, kid. What do you think?"

"Oh." I lifted the book I had found at a second-hand bookstore, *100 Women of Ancient China*, out of my basket. It was filled with illustrations and descriptions of goddesses and influential women in Chinese history. I was searching for new heroines. The quiet mousy girls waiting in the wings were beginning to bore me.

"What's that?" Mouse reached for the book. I tried to pull the book away but was not fast enough. He might have been nuts, but I still didn't want him to think I was a baby for reading picture books. He flipped through the pages.

"Wow. This is cool," he said. He fell into one of the lawn chairs in front of the washers and stared intently into the book. He seemed sincere, and genuinely interested, so while our laundry tumbled around and around in the machines, I showed him my favourite characters.

There was *Hua Mulan*, the famous woman warrior who disguised herself as a man to take her father's place in the army. She was revered for her fighting talents in many bloody battles in the field. Nie Yin Niang was just a young girl when a nun took her away and trained her in sword play in a cave for ten years. Upon her homecoming, many corrupt officials mysteriously died. Liang Hongyu led her army into battle, playing a giant war drum to stir their fighting spirit. There were others too, concubines, poets, and empresses, but, naturally, the *kung fu* masters were the most exciting.

We lingered on the drawings of the women. They were only black ink sketches, but they were finely rendered. The artist had painstakingly drawn the women's hair in detail. The empresses wore elaborate styles, their tresses pinned in layers on top of their heads with ornate combs and jewels. Others, like the dancers, also wore trailing locks that lifted delicately as they spun around. Their robes were inked with peonies, lilies, and poppies. The warriors' swords and staffs were embedded with precious gems.

Page after page, Mouse exclaimed excitedly, "That's a beaut!" or "Brilliant!" I never imagined anyone else would think this was as special as I did. When we moved our clothes to the dryers, Mouse launched into a lecture on the Shaolin Monastery and the Buddhist monks.

"*Lang lui*, haven't you ever seen *The Shaolin Temple* with Jet Li?" he asked. When I shook my head, his face widened in surprise

"Girl, you haven't lived," he said and slapped his thigh.

After I folded my clothes and Mouse threw all his things into a yellow garbage bag, I followed him to his place. He lived in one of the other dilapidated old houses in Kensington Market, about three minutes from where I lived. When he pushed the door open, we were greeted by the scent of dirty socks. Pizza boxes were strewn throughout the long hallway. "Watch your step, *lang lui*," Mouse instructed, kicking debris away to clear me a path. "Sorry, my roommates are a bunch of slobs."

I followed him up a wooden staircase to the second floor. We creaked our way up, me still holding my laundry basket. Finally, he turned the knob of one of the closed doors and led me inside. In contrast to the mess in the main house, Mouse's matchbox of a room was immaculate. It was sparsely furnished and had wood crates all lined up against the wall, stacked neatly on top of each other. He used these crates like art frames, organized to hold similar objects.

I peeked inside of one that contained flat white stones.

Just when I'd been thinking there was a chance he could be sane, his explanation of his room blew that idea to smithereens.

"Snow flakes. From the moon," he said when I picked one up.

In another, he had a pile of feathers. Some looked like they were from a seagull and were long, slender, and white. Others were smaller and plumper in various shades of grey.

"For their curative powers."

There was also a collection of pressed leaves, placed on top of each other neatly, from largest to smallest.

"Books," Mouse said simply. "And pens." He pointed at a neat stack of pine needles.

Throughout the room, Mouse had tied his colourful ribbons to the crates and they looked like flags.

"The ribbons? They're sleeping."

There are many different ways to say "crazy" in Cantonese: *tsaw; hei mong mong; chi seen; deen.* Each word described a particular brand of crazy. *Tsaw* meant "silly." You could say it as a term of affection, as a tease, or as something derogatory or dismissive of someone's inappropriate behaviour. *Hei mong mong* was suited to someone a little foggy, because he was lost in his own world. *Chi seen* was the English equivalent of "crazy," which you shouted when something was outrageous. Then there was *deen*. Well, *deen* meant "certifiable." Locked up crazy. Ma crazy.

That was a lot of words, plenty nuanced, but faced with

all the various forms of recent craziness in my life, I could see there was a need for more words. What I wanted most was one word that would question who the crazy really were — the ones with the off-beat behaviour, or the rest of us for thinking so.

Whether Mouse was *deen* or *tsaw*, he was nice and I, as a new and more reckless Miramar, was in for the adventure of it. I went to sit on his bed. It was perfectly made with a white duvet that was embroidered with pink flowers. It was so delicate and clean, I did not want to muss it up so I just perched on the edge.

Mouse bent down to a small TV with a VHS player beside it. When the film began, he ran over to the bed and jumped on it beside me, bouncing lightly on the mattress like a child. In the movie, Jet Li, a slave to an evil emperor, witnessed the murder of his father. He ran away and was nurtured back to health by a group of monks at the Shaolin Monastery. There he learned integrity, brotherhood, and the noble truths of Buddha. He also learned how to fight because the monks were trained in the secrets of the Shaolin martial arts.

Halfway into the film, I fell hard in love with Jet Li. There was also a fierce shepherdess, the daughter of one of the *kung fu* masters, who gave Jet Li a walloping for killing and roasting her dog for dinner. There was some hint of a romance brewing, but Jet Li decided to embrace her as his sister since he was now a monk.

Mouse's bouncing got more intense during the fight scenes. In the final scene, when the evil warlord waged a battle on the sacred ground of the Shaolin temple, Mouse hopped off the bed and landed in panther pose, Bruce Lee style, his face in a deadly scowl. "EEeeeYoooow. MMMMmmmkicha!" he growled and punched the air.

I had never seen anyone else do air *kung fu* before. Mouse was good, too. I leapt into the mountain stance position, holding my hands at guard. Mouse gave me a nod and we entered into a fight sequence, vanquishing a hundred enemies, just as Jet Li was getting started.

Drums, from the TV, sounded a war song with strong rhythmic beats, which inspired us to accelerate our fight. We kicked at the evil troops, throwing our fists in the air and thrusting the bad guys to death with our imaginary swords. Mouse was an incredible gymnast; he did flips backwards and forwards, always landing in the cat stance before repeating his sequences. I practiced the tiger claw, shattering the clavicle of my imaginary foe. The floor shook. At some point, I worried one of his roommates might get upset, but I did not hear any pounding apart from us, so I forgot about it. Once all of Jet Li's enemies finally lay moaning on the ground, we turned and faced each other, gave a *kung fu* bow and fell laughing to the floor.

When Mouse caught his breath, he said, "Hey! I knew a man from my home village that had the power to stop the earth from moving!" I arched my brow. Home village? Was he a FOB — someone "fresh off the boat?" He did not have any traces of a Chinese accent. I had assumed he was Canadian-born, or, like me, was part of the 1.5 generation.

"Yeah, yeah, yeah," he continued excitedly, flailing his arms. "He could grind the axis of the earth to a halt, and the world would freeze while he rescued villagers from unforeseen misfortune!" He stared at me, waiting for my response, which I wasn't giving him because I was working hard to imagine what he was saying. "Isn't that insane? The world would stand still while you went fast-forward in it!"

Whether Mouse was really *deen* became irrelevant at this point; he was hilarious and I ran with it.

"Whoa," I said. "I can think of a lot of situations when that skill could come in handy." I remembered seeing extraordinary things during the Sunday matinees. I knew that one trained touch could either save a life or end it, and that simple tap could paralyze the entire body. I also learned from Ba that the masters used to travel by way of stepping on the tops of bamboo trees, so light were their feet. But putting the world on freeze-frame? That was a new one.

"I want to learn to do that," he said.

"How do you learn something like that?" I asked.

"Meditation. Start inward and then throw the control outward," he replied.

"I don't get it."

"Well, you have to master yourself. You have to be, within yourself, absolutely calm and peaceful. Then, you'll be able to make the world outside of you just as still," he explained.

"Right." It made sense.

"So, I've been working on it. I meditate every day. Try to empty everything out. Slow my heart rate, breathing, everything. It's almost like you're dead, but not."

I thought about the World Religion class I hadn't finished. We had been learning about Buddha and his enlightenment when I left. "It's a spiritual state of stillness too," I said quietly.

"Go on." Mouse leaned back on the floor, one arm supporting his weight.

I sighed and tried to remember. "Well, maybe, it's about reaching a state of spiritual completeness. Maybe, you aren't even you anymore, you're just part of the whole world. Maybe, then, you can bend time because you are in tune with everything." I got excited as I continued. It was an interesting hypothesis. I remembered getting into such talks with Ba when we would try to unravel the mysteries of the *kung fu* masters' unbelievable powers. He had always leapt right in there with me, never discounting my ideas just because I was a kid.

"And you give up trying to control. You simply become a part of the world. So maybe that guy in your village wasn't really doing it by himself. Maybe the whole universe recognized that what was happening shouldn't happen, and it all worked together in order for him to prevent it. He was just part of the big picture," I felt good, like I'd just realized something.

"Wah. *Lang lui*. I see what you're saying." Mouse let out

a big breath as if he were digesting something profound and was letting it seep slowly into his mind.

As I pieced this hypothesis together, I pictured Ba stepping off the curb. If I had been there, maybe I could have been able to stop time, pluck him out of the line of danger and everything would have been different. Maybe Sophia and Darwin would have turned out to be just regular kids, and I would have finished university. Maybe Ma would have learned to be happy. I felt my heart loosen a bit. It was a lot of maybes.

My eyes got hot. I jumped up. "I gotta go."

Mouse roused himself out of his thoughts. "Really? You don't want to get something to eat? Talk more *kung fu?*"

"No, really, I have to go." I picked up my laundry basket.

"Okay. Hold on, I'll see you out."

I went first down the stairs, clutching my laundry basket, and carefully stepping over the garbage. I let myself out through the door.

"Hey, *lang lui,* wanna watch another film, sometime?" Mouse called from the threshold.

I turned just before reaching the sidewalk. He was leaning against the door frame, a big smile on his face. He reminded me of a cat. A sleek, agile young tomcat. But he was kind and sincere. And cool. I realized I liked him.

"Okay. Sure," I said and shrugged. I pretended to be casual as I walked away but I was shaking a little on the inside.

Chapter 24 ⚭

Ah-Lam knew she was not like the other girls. When they went down to the shore to do their laundry, the others sang together in perfect harmony. Their sweet voices travelled through the fields to where the men worked, causing them to pause and thank the heavens for being alive. When Ah-Lam joined in, her voice screeched like an owl's and the girls, startled, would shoot her dirty looks. Ah-Lam longed for a day when she could afford her own washer and dryer.

IT HAD BEEN FOUR MONTHS since I had run away from my life, and I had not called Ma or Sophia or even Darwin to tell them what I had done or where I was. I needed more time. I wanted to be fully settled into my new life first. They would have questions that I didn't have answers to.

But I was lonely. It was early summer again, and the trees were filled with young leaves. Toward evening, the sky would be filled with purple light, and all around, one could hear mothers calling their children home for dinner in several languages. On one of those beautiful evenings, with the breeze blowing gently through my window, I called Nida. She was home from university for the summer, doing some kind of internship with the TD Bank. Her voice, at once familiar and totally different, was full of exclamation marks.

"Miramar, I thought you had dropped off the face of the earth! Jesus, it's good to hear from you!"

Her voice sounded like home.

"Of course, I want to see you! And guess what, I've talked to Denise and Tina recently. Why don't we all get together? The 4Somes! Want to?"

She had suggested an elegant restaurant in Yorkville. When the night came, I was last to arrive. Among the shining silverware and linen, my friends looked so grown-up. Nida was wearing a blue suit and a crisp white blouse, having just come from work. Her hair cascaded down her shoulders in long, bouncy layers. Denise had on a light jade cardigan over a grey skirt. Tina was clad in a dressy pair of black slacks and black pumps. She had graduated from being a nerd to being a well-dressed, trendy nerd. They looked like kids playing dress-up, but still, I looked down at my jeans and T-shirt and felt left behind.

After the initial hugs and telling each other we looked good, Nida raised her wineglass. "So, ladies. A toast because there is occasion to toast," she said. I lifted my water glass and waited. "I'm engaged!" she trilled.

"Nida!" Denise exclaimed.

"So exciting!" Tina added.

They squealed and reached across the table to hug her. Nida told us she was marrying some boy named Rajiv from Mississauga who also went to Western.

"The wedding will be year after next, when we graduate. Huge. I mean, *huge.* A full on Indian wedding. Like eight hundred guests, my mother estimates. And all the Hindu stuff for the week prior. The *mehndi*, the *marmara*, the whole get-up. You will all be invited, of course. Can you believe it?"

We talked about the wedding for the next half hour. I faked enthusiasm by asking for details. Nida wanted both dresses — the wedding sari for the ceremony and the white gown for part of the reception. Then there would be half a dozen costume changes along with accessories and jewellery, all of which she described in detail. Nida had talked a lot about her future wedding when we were kids. She had planned it, even made lists. The only difference between then and now was that she had always imagined the groom as Ralph Macchio from *The Karate Kid*.

When the fury of the engagement died down, Tina announced that she had just gotten accepted to nursing school, and Denise said she had decided to apply for an MBA. They both had boyfriends, and took out photographs as proof. As they flipped through the pictures, commenting on how hot each others' boyfriends were, I let my posture crumple, feeling more and more like the garden gnome again.

"And you, Miramar? What about you?" Denise asked.

I sat up and tried to brighten. "Oh, I'm good. I left Carleton. It wasn't for me. I may apply somewhere else to finish, but I want to take my time, ya know?" They were all nodding politely while I talked, making me feel shittier and shittier.

"Any man in your life?" Tina asked.

"Well, you know, I'm dating. I haven't met 'the one' yet. But you know, dating is fun. That's where I'm at right now." There was definitely pity on their faces. I began to feel desperate.

"What happened to that guy from North Bay?" Nida asked.

"Oh, him. Whatever. Easy come, easy go." I feigned indifference. I detected an "I told you so" in her tone. She was beginning to get on my nerves.

"How's your family? Sophia? Darwin?" asked Denise cheerily as she handed around the breadbasket.

"They're good. Sophia is in Montreal at McGill. Darwin is in London," I said. At least all these things were true. I hoped my siblings' glamorous lives would make me look slightly more interesting by proxy.

Towards the end of dinner, over a dish of chocolate cheesecake with four forks, Nida said, "Isn't it amazing how well we're all doing?"

Tina and Denise nodded emphatically. We used to be so close. An image of us lip-synching to "How Will I Know" popped in my mind. We had recorded the video, studied it frame by frame, and then taught ourselves the dance moves.

We four had unanimously wanted to grow up to be the Asian Whitney Houston.

Looking around at the faces of my friends, I realized how both familiar and strange they appeared. I had the feeling that this would probably be the last time I ever saw them. I saw how there was no need to try and replicate the 4Somes after this night. A lump started to form in my throat. I was happy for them, I truly was, but I felt as if I had just gotten back from Mars or something, as if my only real news was that aliens do, in fact, exist. And that maybe I was one of them.

Chapter 25 ⌇

*Ai was not sure how she felt about the stranger who had come to
the village. He juggled and told crass jokes, yet his sword skills were
exquisite. Was he a clown or was he a hero? She was in a state of
panic and confusion, having been trained only to fall in love with heroes.*

MOUSE WAS MY FIRST real friend in a long time and a good
distraction from the wandering thoughts that invariably landed me back in quicksand. His enthusiasm for *kung fu* films
gave us a lot to talk about. He did a quick review of my video
collection and quickly added to it. From the Chinatown video
stores, he brought me films with Cheng Pei-Pei, one of the first
major female *kung fu* stars; her legendary *Golden Swallow,*
also known as *The Girl with the Thunderbolt Kick,* went right
on my shelf. "If it's the ladies you want, *lang lui,* you have to
get a load of these girls," he said as he stocked my milk crates
with films feauturing Angela Mao Ying, Lily Li, Karina Wei-
Yin Hung, Michelle Yeoh.

Now, with the summer breeze blowing into my living room,
we disappeared into the ancient landscapes of China — the
cascading waterfalls, weepy willow trees, rolling mountains
— and joined forces with the honourable monks who fought
to protect the temples. We made up storylines, even writing
them down with the intention of sending them off to the Shaw
Brothers, the biggest *kung fu* film studio in Hong Kong. After
work, I could count on Mouse rapping lightly on my door with

gifts of roast pork and barbecued chicken and rice wrapped in wax paper. We would settle into an evening of films and air *kung fu*. I knew Mouse liked me, but I could not tell if he felt any romantic feelings for me. He never made any moves and treated me like his sister. I, however, realized after some time that I was feeling something else. But while the desire to kiss him was building up inside me, I pushed it down, not sure I wanted to unleash that crazy desire again. I shuddered when I thought of the power Jerry had had over me.

One night, a couple of weeks into our friendship, over tin-foil boxes of *chow mein* and *ho fun* noodles, I asked Mouse where he was from.

"*Aiya*, you wouldn't believe me, *lang lui*."

"Try me," I said, as I picked up noodles with my chopsticks.

"I am the spirit of an old gingko tree."

I rolled my eyes. It was hard to talk to Mouse seriously. "Really, huh?" I asked, digging into my bowl.

"Yup. A village grew all around me because they knew I was sacred. They worshipped me, made me offerings, carved my likeness into stone and erected a small shrine at my feet. On festival days, they tied ribbons of every colour to my branches that would fly in the wind."

"Oh, that's where you get your ribbons," I said.

"'Cept I grew ambition," he said with his mouth full.

I rolled my eyes but was secretly loving this. There was no denying Mouse was an excellent storyteller.

"I wanted to escape, but my roots locked me to the earth. I wanted to travel, to see the pink mountains that were far away in the distance. I wanted to reach the top where the clouds shrouded them. I also wanted to go to the sea, to dip my toes in the green water to see if it was cold or warm. But as tall and as wide as I grew, I couldn't reach them."

He shoved a large mouthful of beef and onion *ho fun* into his mouth. I waited for him to go on. "And? What happened?"

"It took many years, maybe a hundred, but finally, I befriended a boy. A strange kid. They called him the 'upside-down' boy because he was always looking up at the sky. Anyway, this boy, Fang, was the only one who could hear my voice, and even though he was mute, I could hear him fine. He was born into the wrong world. Fang's theory was that he was 'sposed to be a spirit, but some mistake had happened. I could believe it too. That kid had eyes like shadows."

I felt the hair on the back of my neck rise. Daniel Greyeyes's face flashed before me.

"So one day, I was telling him about the colour of the sea, the way it changes from blue to green to black as it got deeper. Fang climbed up my branches to see. I told him not to. He wasn't the most coordinated kid on the block, ya know? But he did anyway. He climbed onto one of the tallest branches, gazed out into the sea then spread his arms out like an eagle and went diving down. Next thing I knew, I woke up in his body. A bit scratched up, but in fine shape."

I marvelled at how Mouse was telling me all this as if he were recalling a trip to the grocery store. "Then what?" I implored. This was getting good.

"Then, I took Fang's identity and made the big leap to Gold Mountain. And that, *lang lui*, is where I came from." He ended his story, grinned at me, and heaped more noodles into his bowl. I shook my head. I had to hand it to him. Mouse could really make it as a scriptwriter one of these days. As for getting anything real out of him, that remained to be seen.

"I saw you in Chinatown wearing ribbons once."

"Oh, yeah. It must have been a festival day. I do that sometimes, you know, to remember. Call me sentimental," he said and grinned with his hands spread. Mouse chewed thoughtfully, before asking, "And you, Miss Woo? Where're you from?"

"Scarborough."

"Oh. Cool," he said, moving on to the *chow mein*.

It was already July. Five months since I had spoken to my family. They were probably sick with worry, but as more time passed, I felt less able to call them. I would not be able to handle Sophia's smartassed remarks or Darwin's prolonged silences. Most of all, I didn't want to talk to Ma. Since her rant in the hospital, something seismic had happened in my heart. Our whole lives were a lie. If Ma was not who I thought she was, maybe Ba was not either. Then, I wondered, who was I?

Once upon a time, I thought there were things I could count on, even in times when everything else seemed uncertain. Mouse lived in a tree, longing to be released, while I had lived in a tiny smooth shell, afraid of the shifting sands outside. In some ways, maybe we were both just playing like kids and avoiding the next step. I didn't know what that was for Mouse, but sitting with him on the rug, so full of stories, but also so alone in the world, I knew then that finding my family was mine.

At first, I didn't want to go out with Mouse into Chinatown, in case people thought I was *deen* too. I didn't think I was any more or less kooky than him, but unlike Mouse who saw the world as his theatre, I played out my fantasies in the privacy of my house. But once we ventured out, I relaxed. It seemed that everyone knew him and more importantly, liked him. Or at least, they didn't regard him as a freak. The punk rockers who panhandled in front of the liquor store swapped mixed tapes with him; the *dim sum* servers put out his favourite dumplings before he even had to ask. He greeted all the street hawkers by name, falling into the old village dialect *Toisan* when conversing with the old ladies who sold onions and greens. Mouse also spoke excellent Cantonese to the bosses in the noodle shops. They clapped him on the back like a son.

"*Lui peng-yao?*" one of them asked, looking me up and down, wondering if I was Mouse's girlfriend. I blushed, looking away. Mouse laughed and avoided giving an answer.

Truth be told, it was getting harder to contain the fluttery sensations in my stomach when he came around. I began to notice his arms, the taut slender muscle that ran from his elbow to his wrist. I became familiar with his scent, the smell of earth and rain. His neck curved where it joined his shoulders, and I longed to trace a finger across the turns of his jawline. I loved the sound of his laugh — a tinkling of bells, and the loud, raucous guffaws he made when he was really amused.

I tried to stop it. There would not be enough rocky road ice cream in the world for me to recover from another broken heart. It helped that Mouse stayed neutral as Switzerland toward me. I was his sidekick — the shepherdess to his Jet Li.

Still, sometimes I tread in lightly, put a toe into the water, just to see what would happen. "Why do you call me *lang lui*?" I asked him one night as we were strolling around the neighbourhood. The air was cooling down from a scorching afternoon. It was approaching twilight, and the first star was showing itself in the sky.

"Why not? Aren't you pretty?" he asked.

"Not really. I don't think so," I said.

Mouse stopped walking and turned me to face him. "You're nuts, girl. You're a looker."

"Riiight," I said, pushing by him to keep walking.

"You know what your problem is, Miss Scarborough?" He stayed put on the concrete slab of sidewalk.

"What?" I sighed and turned around.

"You think pretty is all blond and blue eyes and Barbie doll body. That's what all the sisters think growing up in this no-man's land."

I actually liked that he often called Canada "no-man's land," as in no place for people of colour like us. "No, I don't!"

"You," he said, shaping his hands in the air, "are a goddess from the East. Your shining black hair, your almond eyes, your wide cheekbones, your strong calves. You were made to run through fields and rivers like the wind."

"Okay, enough, Mouse. Seriously. Stop." His weird musings were fun when we were dreaming up storylines, but now it felt like he was making fun of me. I started to walk away.

He caught up and stepped in front of me. "Miramar. You are beautiful. I swear." He raised his palm as if making an oath. It was also the first time he had ever said my name.

"Okay, okay," I pushed him away. "Thanks. I guess." We continued walking in silence for a few minutes before Mouse told me his theory on Bruce Lee's one-inch punch while my heart thudded in my chest like a scared rabbit's.

Chapter 26

Wu was accused of treason for fighting in the resistance army and was put in a cell to await her trial. She charmed her way out. No one knew how she did it, but only that she hopped on a horse and rejoined the army the next morning. When asked, she simply said she told the jailer a story. Her story was so powerful that it moved him to tears and uncontrollable laughter. In gratitude, he freed her and gave her a purple ribbon to wear around her sword. She was known as much for her talk-story as for her courage on the battlefield.

MOUSE HAD ALL KINDS of friends. Sometimes, I joined him in the small park in Kensington Market. He liked to hold court on a picnic table, surrounded by people. There was Al the homeless guy who lived in the park. He had a grocery cart filled with his belongings and would spit at anyone who got too close to it. Al didn't speak much. When he did, it was an event.

There was a group of punks who hung around Mouse as well. They were mostly dressed in ripped shirts under studded motorcycle jackets and tattered jeans held together by safety pins. The girls wore black fishnet stockings and Doc Martens laced up to their knees. I was initially nervous around them, but Mouse said, "Punks are good people. It's the skinheads you have to be careful about."

There were also the occasional hippies with long greasy hair, floral skirts, and love beads. They often carried small paperbacks, at times breaking into a recital of poetry or prose.

Sometimes it was Kerouac and other times Ginsberg with an occasional appearance by Walt Whitman, all of which gave me a tingle in the back of my neck.

We spent long afternoons on weekends just hanging out in the park, while kids played in the wading pool and on the jungle gym. Someone always carried a flask filled with mystery booze and passed it around generously, and if there was not any alcohol, there was always weed. The air there was constantly sweet with the smell of it. I refrained from both and was glad to see Mouse did too. He was, as he liked to say, "high on life."

So gathered, Mouse would entertain everyone with his stories. He had lots of them. On one afternoon, one of the punk girls mentioned she was thinking of changing her name. "Like, Sheena, ya know, after the Ramones song?" She was maybe sixteen, with a pink mohawk, black lipstick, and fingernails chewed down to the quick.

"Sheeeee-na," Mouse drawled out the name, looking at the sky. "Yah, I like it. Sheee-na. That's what I'll call you." Sheena smiled, pleased with herself. I could tell she had a crush on Mouse. She sat with one ripped fishnetted thigh pressed against his leg even though there was lots of space on top of the picnic table. I loathed her by whatever name she went by. I sat below them on the bench, eyeing their legs and wondering if Mouse would draw closer to her or pull away. But he stayed where he was, which I didn't know how to read.

"Hey, Mouse, how'd you get your name?" one of the hippies named Stan asked, scratching at his beard.

"I got it when I was working the rails," Mouse began. "Don't cha all know that the Chinaman built your goddamn railroad?" Mouse chastised. There were shakes of the head.

"Well, there's a history lesson in this story, boys and girls." Everyone drew closer. They loved Mouse's stories.

"So the Chinaman was brought over from the old country to build this here Canadian Pacific Railway in Gold Mountain, see? We were cheap. Whites wouldn't do it for the money they

offered, so Sir John A. Macdonald gave us a ring-a-ding."
Mouse held a pretend receiver to his ear. "Hey, how the hell
are you, Mr. Ho-Lee-Chow? We got work. Lots of it. Great
work, great pay, great benefits. C'mon down! You can be the
next contestant on *The Price is Right!*"

Mouse switched his tone. "So here we were. Shit work, shit
pay, no benefits, no four percent holiday pay. No siree, Bob!
Our job was to break rocks so the fire dragon could pass
across the country. The *gweilos* told us we needed to break a
lot of rocks, sometimes even through the mountains." Mouse
leaned towards his audience. "This scared the shit out of us!"
He shouted suddenly making everyone jump. "How the hell
were we gonna break a hole in a mountain? Everyone knew
the mountain spirits were the most powerful of all spirits. You
don't disturb 'em if you know what's what." All eyes were on
Mouse.

"After days of using our sledgehammers, we came to the first
one. Big Mama of all mountains. We were already exhausted
from the back-breaking work. I couldn't even stand up straight!
And that sun! The sun in this new world hated us, man! It
beat on us, shouting for us to get up when we fell down. It
raked through our skin, and burned into our heads. It blinded
our eyes so we made mistakes. Even our tears boiled!" Mouse
wiped his brow for emphasis.

"When we got nearer to the mountain, we got more fucked
up. Some brothas went apeshit crazy. We had to drag them by
the legs along the tracks as we worked because they started
mumbling like babies. The foreman gave us a pep talk, seeing
that we were getting all squirrelly. 'One of you,' he said, 'has
to crawl into a small hole we will make in the mountain and
light a dynamite to blast the rocks apart. Big money,' he said,
rubbing his fat caterpillar fingers together. We knew what dynamite was. It was like a firecracker we had set off on the New
Year but many, many times more powerful. No one wanted to
do it, so I did it. The job required someone small and nimble.

I was the ideal candidate." Mouse paused to take a drag off his cigarette, his eyes squinting in the sun. Everyone waited, breathless, including me.

"I had to, right? The other guys had wives and children back home." Along the picnic table, everyone nodded in understanding.

"So, before I did it, I kneeled in front of mother mountain and asked forgiveness. Punish me later, I said. But not today." Mouse bowed his head.

"The first time I lit the stick, I waited too long. I wasn't sure it was lit. But then, I ran like a motherfucker. As I ran away, I felt small rocks running after me, breaking the skin of my calves. When I got out, I thought it was weird that I could see the other men's mouths moving, but no sound was coming out. Blood was pouring out of my ears. The explosion made me deaf for two days."

Sheena wiped away a tear. Mouse slapped his thighs. "But the foreman decided I was good at it, and that, my friends, is how I got my name. They called me Mouse because I was small and fast. I outran the fire."

"What about the mountain spirits?" one of the hippies asked. She was wide-eyed and her frizzy red hair was a golden halo around her face, making her look like a fairy.

"Haven't got to me yet!" Mouse gave her an ironic grin.

Everyone erupted into applause and pats on the back for Mouse. Al, from behind his grocery cart hollered, "Damn good story!"

I stood back and watched the happy scene, thinking of how much Ba would have liked Mouse. He had always enjoyed a well-told story.

Chapter 27 ⤚

*Zhi was told again and again she was nothing without her family.
"Our name is our honour!" her mother repeated a million times. Zhi
walked a straight line, never wanting to lose face for her family. But
then they all died, and she did not know what that meant for her
face or her name.*

THAT NIGHT I DREAMED about the house in Scarborough. It
was spring and cherry blossom petals were raining onto my
head as I walked around the familiar streets. In place of the
playground where Sophia and I used to love to ride on the
squeaky see-saw, there was a pagoda instead, a sweet stream
of incense wafting out of it like a long, lazy finger. Where the
road should have been, a river meandered, transparent like
glass and filled with gold and red koi. The fish swam beside
me as I walked towards home. Our house was cast in an enormous shadow. The old maple tree towered above it, encircling
everything in its shade. Its trunk was double the size of the
house. As I drew nearer, I realized the house no longer sat on
the ground, but that the tree was carrying it up into the sky as
it grew. Its green leaves fluttered high above my head, a sign I
took to mean it was welcoming me home. In the dream, I felt
really happy, but I awoke with tears on my face.

One night in early August, Mouse and I were drafting yet
another *kung fu* story in my apartment. The day had been a

steamy one, and we sat at my kitchen table with a fan blasting wind at us. The head moved back and forth from me to him and back again. We had sent three scripts to The Shaw Brother Studios already, paying hefty postage for the two-hundred page manuscripts to Hong Kong. This one was going to be a contemporary tale set in a Chinatown somewhere in the West. We would keep the conventional storyline — vengeance, good against evil — but with an urban twist.

"So I was thinking we could do a large family — lots of brothers and sisters. Mother and father are in exile from China for some reason — probably political. They are actually martial arts experts who secretly train their kids in the basement of their house, preparing for the day when they will go back and liberate the people from military rule. Cool, eh?" He was smoking cigarette after cigarette, the smoke shattered by the blasts of air from the fan. There had been a mass uprising in Beijing that summer. Students had occupied Tiananmen Square, pushing the government for democracy. Mouse and I had watched the TV in disbelief when the tanks were sent in and bodies fell in the streets. Mouse had fallen into a heavy mood for a couple of days as if his own family had shed blood in the square. I wondered whether his family was actually there, but I didn't want to ask. I did not want him to make up another story. I needed either the truth or nothing.

"Nah. Orphan. That works better. Alone in the world, that kind of thing," I said, gnawing on the end of my pen.

"Again with the orphans! We've already written two stories with orphans." Mouse jumped to his feet, pacing between the stove and the fridge. "No. A family of warriors. Each person with his own specialty. Crane dance. Drunken staff. Lion fist. First, they encounter skinheads who have been extorting money from Chinatown, see, then…"

"Orphan, Mouse."

"Jesus H. Christ! What's your obsession with orphans? Are you one?" He pointed his cigarette at me like an accusation.

I paused and felt my heart drain. I was not an orphan, entirely, only by half. Ma was still alive. And I still had my siblings. I just didn't know if they all hated me for leaving them. Maybe they did and I was actually all alone in the world. Maybe that was what I wanted, why I could not make myself rejoin my family, the family I still had left.

"Hellooooo. Earth calling Miramar Woo?" Mouse waved a hand in front of my face.

I blinked. "No, Mouse. I am not an orphan."

"But you had to think about it? What is it with you?" He sat back down, tapping cinders into the soy sauce dish I let him use as an ashtray.

I got up from the floor and went into my bedroom. What I wanted to do was shut the door and go to bed, but instead I went to the bottom of a pile of textbooks where I had put the scrapbook. I went back out to the living room and handed it to him.

He opened it to the first page where I had written in bold black marker: SOPHIA AND DARWIN WOO. He turned the pages slowly. There were black-and-white photographs and newspaper articles documenting their appearances and performances. Toward the middle, I had also clipped the glossy colour feature published in *Maclean's Magazine* a year earlier. There was a photo of Darwin giving the peace sign on a stage. Another was of Sophia, smiling into the camera as a group of white-haired professors surrounded her in a semi-circle. There was also a photo of Ma, with one arm around Darwin in front of Carnegie Hall. Much smaller, beneath this, was an image of all of us at Niagara Falls. Ba was wearing his fishing cap and we were all smiling broadly.

"This is your family?" Mouse asked me, looking up from the pages.

"I'm no orphan," I said.

"But it says here that your dad died." He traced the line in the *Maclean's* article with a finger.

"Ba got hit by a car." He looked up at me again. I did not feel anything when I said it.

"And your brother and sister are gifted, huh?" He scratched his head.

"I guess so," I sighed.

"Do you see them a lot?"

"No. They don't even know where I am."

"How come?"

"I don't know."

"Does your mother know where you are?"

"No," I said.

"Then you're kinda like an orphan," Mouse said slowly.

"Hmmm. There is reason in what you say, little grasshopper," I said, trying to be funny, but Mouse just looked at me.

A silence engulfed us, travelling like the streams of smoke from Mouse's cigarette. I ached right then from my muscles up through to my skin. I needed someone to hold me, to remind me that I was still human, that touch still mattered. But I stood where I was and he kept flipping through the pages until there were no more. Then he gently handed me the book.

"Hey, kid. No worries." He hopped up and slapped me on the back on his way to the kitchen. "You've got me. Besides, you're right, *kung fu* heroes are usually orphans. They've got no family. What was I thinking? We're just a travelling band of orphans, gathering each other up, inventing our own identities and making new families as we go, right?"

I heard the tap running. "You want some water?" he called out.

Soon sweaters replaced T-shirts and sneakers banished sandals. Toronto was a city of abrupt contrasts; the warmer seasons brought out patios and a street life that coloured the days and nights with people. As it got cooler, the population appeared to diminish little by little until it was as if the place were a grey-stained ghost town.

In September, Mouse got a bartending job in the evenings, so I didn't see him as much. Occasionally, I would wake up to the sound of pebbles peppering the glass of my window late in the night and I would look out to see Mouse underneath holding up bags of takeout. He would come after his shifts at the bar, full of energy to write out new storylines he had come up with for our projects. On the mornings after, I would go to work half-asleep, counting the minutes before I could go home and climb back into bed. My boss, the woman with the gold-rimmed glasses, strangely enough, seemed to approve of my dishevelled state.

"Looks like you've gone out and got yourself a life, Miramar. Good for you. Youth is not to be wasted, my dear," she told me. Regardless of how raggedy I appeared, she seemed satisfied with my job performance. My numbers were good. The immigrants were getting what they needed. Little did she know I was making up my own system as I went along. Someone needed housing? I pretended to be a former landlord and gave them the referral. Needed Canadian experience for a job? I put on my best manager voice and offered glowing reviews. It was not lying. I was simply doling out poetic justice, making minor adjustments to the topsy-turvy world that had one end slipping quickly over the edge while privileging the other end with too much gravity.

The thought of calling my family had been sitting in my stomach like a little stone. I even imagined the full script for how it would go down. I would call Sophia first, and she would tell me how Ma and Darwin were doing. Then I might call Ma. Maybe. One day I even went so far as to punch in the numbers on the phone, but I hung up before I got a connection. As always, I continued to look for news about them in magazines, in concert listings in the UK papers, but weirdly, there was nothing.

Until recently, despite the months we had not seen each other or talked, I still felt an invisible cord tying us together. At least I could keep up with them in print, see their faces, know where they were. Yet that fall, with no contact in any way, I felt the cord thinning, ready to break.

Chapter 28 ~

Hua steered her horse towards the hills, tearing through the tall grass as the Bandit King rode beside her. She was surrounded by the wind striking her face and the smell of an approaching spring rain. The yellow ribbons tied to her arm fluttered like tails. She glanced at her beloved and saw his face, tilted to the swirling clouds above. Like him, she was born to be wild.

ONE DAY AT WORK, I was with my client Mary Chan and was just about to make a call to her boss as her lawyer. She worked at a garment factory, a.k.a., a sweatshop, and she and her co-workers were trying to unionize, which, once word had gotten out, expediently led to several firings. Mary Chan, who must have been close to my age, passed her giant, round-faced baby from thigh to thigh, jiggling her legs to keep the kid from crying. Meanwhile, her three-year-old roamed freely around my office, pulling books and files off the shelves while singing a broken, "Row, Row, Row Your Boat."

As I was preparing my lawyer voice, the phone rang. It was Mouse. Lately, my feelings for Mouse were getting stronger. Whenever I heard his voice or he walked through my door, my hands would sweat and my heart would take off running. I was so afraid he would notice that I started avoiding him. But the more I made excuses not to see him, the more he persisted. Lately, I had noticed him looking at me while I was at work on our screenplays. I didn't know what to make of it, but I didn't dare hope that he was beginning to feel something for me too.

"Hey, *lang lui*, what are you doing tonight? Come meet me at the bar."

"I don't know, Mouse. I have to work early tomorrow morning."

"You won't regret it. There's someone I want you to see."

"Who?" The chubby baby was smiling at me, her eyes bright as moons.

"She's a vampire. Or at least that's what she tells everyone. She's got this white skin, like fucking whiter than white. These intense violet eyes. I was thinking, we should write a ghost story next. *Kung fu* ghosts, ya know. She would make a great character."

"I dunno. We'll see." I reached my hand out to grab a fleshy hand. The baby giggled.

"Okay, just come." His voice took on a more serious tone than I was used to. "Please, come."

Dusk bar was a short walk from my house on Augusta Avenue in Kensington, not far from Chinatown. I really liked Kensington Market, liked its story, its evolution: once a Jewish enclave in the early 1900s, it then hosted a succession of other Eastern Europeans, Italians, and Portuguese. Ba used to bring us there after films at the Golden Harvest Theatre to get fresh chickens when you could still buy live animals. Now it was changing with cafés and vintage clothing stores, but if you knew where to look, there were some of the best ethnic grocery stores in the city, and peeking out from between shops, a synagogue or two. I took note of where they were, in case Sophia was still considering becoming Jewish.

I started walking to Dusk around eleven p.m., passing the darkened doors of the bodegas, the clothing shops and other bars. The streetlights cast an orange sheen onto the empty sidewalk. As I passed, rats feasting on the day's garbage scurried away. Forget potential rapists or muggers—the thought of a rat clambering over my shoe freaked me out the most. I ran the rest of the way.

The bar used to be a dried goods store, and yellowed boxes of beans still lined the window. I descended a flight of stairs and fumbled for the door in the dark. Inside was an enormous dark room with low ceilings; its only illumination came from lines of Christmas lights that zigzagged across the walls and candles that sat on tabletops. There was music — slow, sad music that went straight to my heart. People dressed in dark clothing were dancing, weaving through one another in the centre of the floor. At one end of the space was a small empty stage and at the other was a bar lined with bottles. People sat on short stools there, and talking to them from behind the bar was Mouse, a fog of smoke hovering above him.

"Hey, *lang lui*, over here," Mouse waved at me, then hopped over the bar. Beside me, he said loudly into my ear, "What do you think?" He spread his arms to make a sweep of the place.

"It's nice," I nodded.

"D'ya wanna drink?"

I felt awkward standing in the middle of the dance floor among the shadowy dancers although I was happy to note I blended in nicely with my all black outfit. "Not right now. Thanks."

"You wanna dance?"

I stared at him. Only Mouse would get a job so relaxed he could decide to be a patron in his own bar. "Don't you have to work?"

"Mikey's covering for me." He gestured with his thumb at the bar to a man who was dressed in nothing but leather chaps and a codpiece. Mikey nodded to me while he sipped at his glass with a straw.

Mouse jogged towards the stage and hopped on. We had never danced together before. Air *kung fu*, certainly, but dancing, never. The music switched to a slightly fast beat, the sound of a bass guitar drifted from the speakers like rising smoke. I recognized the first chords of The Cure's "Lovesong." Mouse started to sway back and forth in time to the singer's melancholic drawl, his body moving like a pendulum.

Head down, Mouse stepped left to right to left on the stage, his arms folded across his chest, instantly lost in the music. A scatter of people danced below on the floor. This was not real life, down here in the dark. I wanted to be with him, moving beside him. I climbed the one big step onto the platform just as the song quickened. Mouse did not even look up. He just took my hands and spun me around and around as the beat became more frenzied. I saw tiny dots of light stream past me as we whirled together faster and faster, the neon and music and air breaking into strobes, into fragments.

This was not real. It was a dream.

The song neared its end, and Mouse drew me to him in an embrace. We rocked gently against each other, finding our rhythm as we moved. I buried my head in Mouse's shoulder, inhaling the scent of smoke and pine. I felt light, like I could just drift off into the air and fly above all these people, and into the night.

I lifted my head to his face. He looked at me for a second and then gently, he pressed his lips to mine. That pretty mouth was so soft it was like being kissed by a flower. I laid my head back on his shoulder.

"You okay?" Mouse whispered.

"Yah, Mouse. I'm okay."

That night, we awkwardly arranged and rearranged our limbs around each other on my bed. Earlier it had been warm, so I had opened all the windows, but now a chilly breeze blew through the apartment. I was shy being naked in front of him. Mouse was all lean brown muscles and smooth skin, and I felt too soft, too pale, too goose-pimpled, too clumsy. When he pressed his mouth between my legs, my body quaked. When he came, it was with a loud wail, like a low siren passing. Afterwards, Mouse wrapped his arms around me and we slept.

After that, not much changed except he had his own key to my apartment and came over almost every night after his shift. Sometimes, I went to the bar and hung out there until closing time. We still plotted our *kung fu* stories, writing them down in storyboard form, riffing off of each other's crazy ideas, and we still did air *kung fu* the same, the only difference being that after the big fight scene, we would collapse on top of each other on the floor and make out.

We never said we were boyfriend/girlfriend. I knew this was not going to be a Nida and her Rajiv from Mississauga kind of romance. And yet, it felt like the easiest thing in the world.

Chapter 29

Na was happy in her new life among the nomads. They had given her shelter when she became lost looking for her father and brothers who had been captured by the magistrate's men. She became their shepherdess because she liked her solitude. On still nights, while the roaming sheep slept, she felt a longing for home and searched the dark outline of the mountain range for a sign of familiarity. Frustrated, she danced the crane as her mother had taught her. Na's frenzied movements scattered the sleeping birds from their trees, and they complained loudly as they flew away. Na continued her dance, thinking to herself, so "this is what it sounds like when doves cry."

ON CHRISTMAS EVE, instead of takeout food, Mouse decided to cook us a turkey. When he brought it over, I was afraid the oven that I never used would be too small for it. We were relieved when it slid in with barely a centimetre clearance on all sides. All day, Mouse had hummed to himself as he chopped and basted. I never even knew he could cook. Since I hardly knew anything about his past, he remained full of surprises. I turned the dial on the radio, looking for something appropriate for us to listen to. I settled on a jazz station, and bluesy Christmas carols filled my apartment while a heavy snow fell outside, covering the dirt of the streets.

Now that it was December, I knew my time was running out. I had made a pinky promise to Darwin — every Chinese New Year, no matter what. Even if he despised me and disowned me as his sister, a pinky promise was a promise. With Mouse in the kitchen, and the sound of a knife hitting the cutting board solidly, and the scraping of a spoon against a plastic bowl, and the sizzle of onions hitting hot oil, I was slipping into emotions I had tried to tuck away in the hopes that they would not surface for a while.

I wondered what my family was doing. Christmas did not have the expectation for us as it had for our white friends. We had tried it on, though, like a borrowed sweater, and we had to admit the little emblems of the holiday were fun: there was the silver tinsel tree Ma bought because it would not drop needles on the carpet and was virtually self-decorating. "A savings!" Ma had said. And it had been fun to open up gifts of new snow boots or mitts. Sometimes, Darwin got a toy — Lego one year, and *Star Wars* figures when he got older. But only once had Ma tried baking a turkey. All our neighbours did it, so Ba had brought one home. It looked like an oversized chicken. Despite Ma's ample skill in the kitchen, the bird had turned out to be a leathery old thing. We made a good attempt at chewing until our jaws had become sore and we had to give up. Ma had actually made a fantastic turkey congee with the carcass, I recalled, but still we never tried turkey again, sticking instead with duck for special occasions.

But Chinese New Year we did not mess around with. It was who we were.

When Mouse presented the meal to me, I thought I would cry or laugh or both. His turkey looked like it came out of the pages of *Good Housekeeping Weekly*. "How'd you learn to do that?" I asked, stupefied. He was even carving it expertly.

"Here and there. I've worked in restaurants and picked up a few things," he answered.

Mouse had laid a white cloth on the worn surface of my second-hand table. On it was rice, steaming yellow with nuts and bits of vegetables. A blue bowl of Chinese greens sat beside it, gleaming with oil and speckled with garlic. In another larger bowl were mashed potatoes with pads of butter melting slowly into pools. Another platter held crackers and different blocks of cheese and olives. There was corn on the cob, green peas, cranberry sauce, and gravy the colour of caramel. It was enough food for the Waltons, the Cosby kids, and the Brady Brunch, if they ever got together and had one whacked-out communal meal.

"Holy Mother of God!" I exclaimed.

"That she was. Happy Birthday, Jesus." He smiled and raised his glass of wine. "This is what I like to call a multicultural smorgasbord," Mouse said, between chews, pointing at the food. "A bit of *biryani*, a bit of *choi*, a bit of *gweilo* mashed potatoes, and a whole lot of poultry."

"I like this smorgasbord thing!"

We made barely a dent in the feast before I found myself having to stop for a break. Good thing I was wearing elastic-waisted sweatpants. Mouse refilled my wineglass.

"You like, *señorita*?"

"I love it!"

"Great! My job is done."

I did not want to say anything, and even suspected it might not be a smart move, but I felt compelled. "Why aren't you with your family today? I assume you come from someone, somewhere?" I asked.

He smiled lazily. "Don't you remember, I was the spirit of a gingko —"

"Stop!" I said. "Not again with the tree. Where's your family?"

He shrugged and concentrated on sucking the meat off the turkey neck.

"What happened? I mean, did something happen to them?"

When I saw his face, it was clear I had stepped too far. "Hey, Miramar? I don't bug you about your family, so don't bug me about mine, deal?"

I was taken aback by the edge in his voice. I had never heard him speak like that before. He was still working on his turkey, but irritation lined his forehead.

"Okay, I guess I was just trying to get to know you better. I mean, I really don't know much about you."

Mouse dropped the turkey onto his plate. "So you feel like you don't know me?" He looked me in the eye. There were licks of fire in his.

"Well, I mean ... not about your past. Like, where did you grow up? Do you have brothers and sisters? What school did you go to? I just wanted to know...." I really did not understand why it was such a big deal. I was not exactly forthcoming about my personal life, but this was ridiculous.

"Do you have to know those things in order to know me? You already know me better than anybody. It pisses me off that you feel you don't know me," he said, reaching for his pack of cigarettes, the turkey forgotten.

"Okay. Sorry I asked. I didn't mean that I don't *know* you. I just wanted to know more, that's all." I brushed it off. Now that I knew what the reaction would be, it seemed Mouse, like his name, would have to remain an elusive thing.

I was glad when our spat was over, and after dinner, we sat cross-legged on the parquet floor of my living room, listening to a CD of *Yellow River*, a classical Chinese piece. After some cigarettes, more turkey and a lot more wine, our conversation about family seemed forgotten, and Mouse returned to his normal self.

Out of his jean pocket, Mouse dug out a red silk box. "Merry Jesus' Birthday," he said. "I know it's a *gweilo* holiday and all, but I wanted to give you something." He was almost blushing. I was touched. I flipped open the lid and found a jade pendant, carved into a lotus flower. It was pale green, but darker towards the middle. A red silk cord was strung through it.

I touched it delicately with my fingers.

"Put it on," Mouse said. He took the pendant from me and

draped it over my head. I looked down at it, my eyes lightly misting over. "The longer you wear it, the greener it'll get."

"I love it, Mouse." I leaned over and kissed him on the cheek. Then I jumped over to the closet where I had hidden his present. I took out a wrapped box. The paper was covered with floppy-eared puppies in red Santa hats. A giant green bow tied it all together. "Ta da!"

"For me?"

"Well, it being a *gweilo* holiday and all, if you don't want it, I can always take it back," I joked. He grabbed it from my hand and pulled it open at the taped seams so as to not rip the paper. It was a video of *Return of the 5 Deadly Venoms,* a cult classic that wasn't easy to find. I had implored the shopkeeper at the video store to order it from Hong Kong for me several weeks ago. He had finally consented, after I offered him an extra twenty bucks for his troubles.

"Woohoooooo!" Mouse yelled, his fists pumping the air. Then he picked me up and twirled me around, staggering a bit.

"Thanks, *lang lui*," he said, hugging me. Then he kissed me on the lips. His lips were warm velvet, cushioning my mouth like a pillow. "Hey. You're the best," he added, his arms still tight around my waist.

"Thanks," I smiled. I could have said other things like how I was in love with him. We could have let words make solid this sweet space between us. But we could not even look at each other in the eye, and instead we started swiping at each other until it became a full tickle fest and I was trapped under him, laughing until I thought I would puke. Then he kissed me again, and we found our way back to each other without all the words and the complications they brought.

Later, I was glad we didn't say it because I wasn't sure what love meant anymore. Love was like a calm lake when all was well; it was nice to watch the sun catch ripples of water and send up flashes of extraordinary light. But if you broke the surface and went deep, it became this thick and murky thing.

Chapter 30 ⚞

Wen's sifu had told her that a true warrior knows the difference between right and wrong, honour and disgrace, truth and lies. But Wen found it much harder to discern these things than it was to decide whether to use fire staff or the precious plum fists when facing an opponent who employed the tiger claw.

IT WAS FOUR DAYS before the lunar New Year in 1990, and all day, I had mentally prepared myself. I had officially run out of time, and it had to be now or never. At work, half my mind was occupied with the conversations that awaited me. The other half tried to dig myself out of the anxiety and get some work done. I wanted the day to drag, for the minutes to turn into hours, but instead, they sped by and before I knew it, I was on the streetcar heading home along with the other grey winter faces of my fellow commuters. I looked from one tired body to another, wondering what they were going home to. The windows of the streetcar were awash with salt and dirt, making it impossible to look outside or for light to shine in. But at five p.m. in January, there was hardly any light in the sky left anyway. I left my house every morning in partial daylight and arrived home in partial darkness. I appreciated the metaphor.

I had no appetite for dinner. I tried to talk myself into feeling calm, convincing myself that a one-year absence wasn't a big deal, and that Sophia, Darwin, and Ma would not be angry with me. I imagined Sophia's face when she picked up the phone — her elation at my voice. Maybe she would cry a little and tell me she had missed me.

I realized, as I did all I could to delay the call, that I missed them. I missed Sophia's wayward eye. I missed Darwin's pranks. I missed Ma. Whoever she was, she was my mother, and I missed her. For most of the year apart, I had simmered in a stew of hate, resentment, and betrayal, but of course, that was childish. She had raised me; she was my Ma. There were no memories of Ba, or any of us, if there was no Ma.

I pressed Sophia's number in Montreal, willing myself not to hang up before someone answered.

"Allo?" The person on the other end said softly.

"Hello. May I speak to Sophia Woo, please?"

"Sophie doesn't live here anymore." The woman sounded surprised.

"Oh. I see. Do you know where I can reach her?" My heart, which had been beating too fast already, quickened.

"She went back to Toronto. Who is calling, please?"

"It's ... uh ... I'm ... her sister, Miramar," I stammered, embarrassed that this woman would know that I had no clue where my sister was.

"Miramar!" she gasped.

"Yes." I was really nervous.

"They've been looking for you. Everywhere. Oh dear! You must call them. Please wait. I'll get the number." I heard high heels clacking against a hard surface. It grew distant and came back again.

"They are in Toronto. It's 503-4902. Do you have a pen? Are you writing this down?" Her voice was full of concern. Iris. That was her name. I remembered now. How much Sophia adored her.

"Yes, thank you for your help."

"Please, Miramar. Whatever is happening with you, please call them," she said.

I replaced the receiver, but did not remove my hand from it. This was the number of our house in Scarborough. Why was Sophia not in Montreal? I picked up the phone again and dialled Darwin's residence in London.

"Hello?" A man answered sleepily after five rings. I suddenly realized it was two a.m. in London.

"I'm so sorry to be calling so late. I wanted to speak to Darwin Woo, please. It's his sister."

"Darwin? Darwin left us some months ago. Is everything all right?" I could tell he was wide awake now. He spoke with clipped deliberateness, reminding me of the voice that had narrated all the nature shows I used to watch as a kid.

"Oh, no, nothing is wrong. I'm so sorry. Can you tell me where he is?"

"He's in Toronto, I presume. I really don't know. I'm the headmaster here."

"Oh, yes, thanks. I remember now. Right. He's in Toronto. I'm so sorry to have disturbed you. Thank you." I hung up before he could say another word.

Something was deeply wrong. I had prepared myself for a very specific range of scenarios, but I was not expecting this. I fingered the scrap of paper on which I had written my own home number. The sequence of numbers stared back at me, like a secret code.

Mouse found me several hours later, still sitting on the floor with the paper in my hand.

"*Lang lui*, what're you doing? Meditating? Summoning the Eight Immortals? What's up?" He ruffled my hair.

"I called my sister."

He dropped to the ground beside me. "Wah. Heavy."

"Yeah, but she's not there anymore. My brother's not in London either. They're home. In Scarborough."

"What're you gonna do?"

"I don't know." We stared at each other for what seemed

like a long time.

"I think I have to call them." I glanced at my watch. It was already past midnight. "Will you stay here with me while I call?" I asked Mouse. He nodded.

I punched in the numbers and waited while it rang. On the third ring, Sophia answered.

"Hello?"

For a moment, I thought about hanging up, but I steeled myself to speak. "Sophia? It's me."

There was a long pause. "Miramar?" And then louder, "Miramar?"

"Yes. It's me," I repeated, twirling the phone cord around my fingers.

"Where are you? What happened to you?"

"I'm in Toronto."

"Why didn't you call us? Why didn't you tell us?" Her voice got clogged up. She was crying.

"Sophia, I'm sorry. I'm sorry." It was all I could think of to say.

"I don't want … I can't talk to you." She hung up.

I replaced the receiver, my eyes filling up. The guilt was unbearable. I had held it off for a year and now it was gathering itself to bury me.

"She hung up?" Mouse asked, his hand on my shoulder.

I nodded.

"Are you okay?"

"No."

"You want something to eat?"

"No!" I screamed. Mouse leaned back, startled.

"Okay, fine. Sorry," he said, slowly getting up.

I picked up the phone again and dialled. This time it rang for a long time. Finally, she picked up. "Miramar, stop calling!"

"Sophia, tell me what's going on. Why are you there? Where's Darwin? Ma?" I spoke quickly, before she could hang up again.

"Why do you care? You left us." Sophia wasn't crying anymore. There was blood in her voice.

"Please, Sophia. Tell me what's happening-"

"I'm here because I lost my Gift, okay? And Darwin, too. We're both at home now because no one gives a shit anymore. And Ma? You want to know where Ma is? She's back in the hospital. She went fucking nuts again. Happy, Miramar? Are you happy now?" she screamed into the phone.

I was crying hard now, and I wiped away my snot with the back of my hand, trying to take it all in. "Are you all right? Is Dar, is he all right?"

"Am I all right? What the hell do you think? I've been a fucking circus monkey for the past two and a half years and now I can't add two and two together. I'm sitting here in fucking Scarborough wondering how I'm gonna raise Darwin, get Ma out of the hospital and whether my fucking sister is alive or dead. What do you think?"

I deserved it. Or maybe I deserved it. I did not know.

"Can I come see you guys? Can we talk? Please."

"No. I don't know. I have to think about it."

I accepted a tissue from Mouse. "Can I call you back tomorrow? Is that enough time for you to think?" There was another long silence. I thought maybe she had hung up again.

"Yeah, call me tomorrow," she sighed and hung up.

Mouse was in the kitchen, getting a bowl for his takeout. I went to the kitchen to apologize for snapping at him. I kept ruining it with everyone who mattered. "Sorry, Mouse. I didn't mean to—"

"Forget about it. S'okay." He patted me on the back. "Mind if I eat?"

"Nah." I watched him spoon *mau pao tofu* onto a bowl of rice.

"Hey, *lang lui*, if this is causing you so much stress, why don't you just drop it?"

"What do you mean?"

"I mean, you seem like you're doing okay without your

family. Why dig up old wounds? I mean, I don't know what happened between y'all, but maybe let sleeping dogs lie, ya know?" He opened the drawer to get chopsticks.

"Are you kidding me? My family's in trouble. Like really serious trouble. You think I should just abandon them?"

"Well, I mean they're in trouble with you or without you, right?"

"So, just disappear. Pretend I never had a family?"

"Yah, I guess. I mean, you make your own family as you go, right? You know, it's like in *Heroes of the East*. Remember how that guy, what's his name, Ah Wing or something, left because his father was nagging him to be a woodcutter like him? And then he realized he was really a poet? And then he met up with the bandits and he joined them and—"

"Are you crazy?" Anger burst from me like a long-smouldering volcano. "We're not talking about the films. We're talking about my family!"

"Okay," he nodded, trying to get by me. My volcano was past polite. It was steaming and boiling over all my frustration, loss, and want. And all of it was flooding out at once.

"What the hell do you know about it anyway? You're a goddamn tree, right?"

For a moment, Mouse just stared at me. His face was a mask I could not read. Only a small twitch of his mouth revealed I had hit a nerve. Finally, he said so quietly I could almost not hear him, "Then go home. What are you waiting for?"

I wanted to kick, to smash something. "You can't deal with the real world, can you? You really can't," I shouted.

Mouse turned and flung the bowl he was holding against the kitchen wall. It shattered, rice falling like rain. "What does that have to do with anything? At least I have a life. I have friends. You don't have any friends. Just me. So what does that make you, Miss Real Fucking World?" He strode into the living room and grabbed his coat from the floor.

I wanted him to be angry. I needed him to be as angry as I

was. And I wanted to scream harder and louder, than I ever had. "And who are you, anyway? Do you even know anymore? You're so far gone, you probably don't even remember your real name." I could not stop. The lava of my heart continued to sputter as he pulled on his coat.

"Tell me! What's your real name?" I screamed as he slammed out of the apartment.

Chapter 31 ⌐⌐

The drums sounded and were reaching a crescendo. The time of reckoning was now. Yan walked through the soldiers lined up on both sides and prepared to enter the palace to face her fate. Would she be welcomed or punished? It was anyone's toss.

I DID NOT SLEEP that night. I did not deserve sleep. It would serve me right if I never slept again. After Mouse left, I turned off all the lights and dropped to the floor and stayed that way for hours. If I didn't move, perhaps no further damage could be done. Perhaps it could even be reversed and the earth could retain its equilibrium. Sophia and Darwin would regain The Gifts, Ma would collect her senses, Ba would return from the dead, and Mouse could happily go on just being Mouse. I would continue to lie on that floor until I crumbled into the tiniest grains of dust and blew away.

I had abandoned my family, and now they hated me. Ba would have been so disappointed. He had always believed in me, knew that no matter what, I would be a rock for my family. And I had blown it. I thought for a change that I deserved to look out for myself, to try and make myself into someone, to forge a new heroic life. I was full of shit. I had not forged anything except ruin. I had wrecked everything I loved, and was back to worse than where I had started. I was weak; I was small. Now I was worse than average. I was a coward too.

While I lay on the cold living room floor, I was pummelled with a million dream-like images. I was five, and Ba taught me how to swim in the sea at Lantau Island. I was scared, but Ba held my hands as I learned to float. My head underwater, I opened my eyes and saw his feet, toes sunk in the sand. I panicked and inhaled the salty water. What was I so afraid of?

I was seven, and Ba brought Sophia and me to the hospital to see Ma and Darwin. Ma lay against the white pillows, her hair spilling over her shoulders. She held Darwin in her arms, and wore the most beautiful smile I had ever seen on her face. *Come closer*, she told us. Sophia and I, on either side of Ma, looked down at our baby brother, his face wrinkled and red like a raisin. We stroked his arms, and Darwin grabbed onto our fingers and held tight.

I was nine. We were boarding the plane in Hong Kong. I saw my grandparents, aunts, and uncles waving at us from the terrace of the airport as we climbed the stairs onto the flying machine. My eyes were pulled in these two directions — the giant airplane in front of me and my grandmother's pained face, tears streaming down her cheeks. All the while, I felt Ba's hand against my back, guiding me forward.

I was thirteen. It had snowed for days, the banks had grown taller than us. School was cancelled. Ma told the three of us to get in our snowsuits and play in the backyard. To keep Darwin entertained, Sophia and I pretended to work in a candy factory, breaking pieces of icicles into bits and sprinkling them with snow. When Ba got home that night, we presented our parents with a Frisbee tray of our creations for dessert. Ma and Ba made *ooommmm* noises as they pretended to eat our snow cakes, and Darwin hopped from foot to foot in delight.

As the first sign of light crept into the living room, I got up from the floor and went to the bathroom to clean my face. My body ached and my eyes were almost glued shut from dried tears.

I went to the kitchen to make coffee and cut my toe on a shard of the bowl that had shattered all over the kitchen. "Ow." I hopped back to the bathroom on one foot to get a bandage. I should not have lashed out at Mouse. It was my problem that I had cast my family out, not his. Mouse had only been good to me. And now he was gone too. It wasn't that I didn't have a past. I was making sure I had no present.

After my foot was fixed and coffee drunk, it was still early, only seven-fifteen a.m., but I could not wait anymore. I called Sophia.

She picked up on the first ring. "Hey," she answered.

"Hey." For a moment, we were silent, but I could feel a familiar current tingling in my body. It was the feeling of returning home.

We didn't say much. She didn't seem angry anymore, just resigned and tired. I said I would come immediately and she didn't argue.

After I hung up, I surveyed the damage in the kitchen, the broken bowl, the grains of rice all over the black and green tiles, the smear of sauce on the wall. It might be the last thing Mouse left me, and I wanted to remember what I did to him. I turned away from it. Let broken things lie.

Riding the subway across the Bloor line to Kennedy, I got itchier; I felt so purely happy to be going home it did not even matter how I might be received. The car rumbled as it pushed through the dark tunnels to the outside, showing us riders in a sudden burst of sunlight. High-rises began to dominate the scenery, a telltale sign that the suburbs were nearing. I waited for a bus at the subway station, checking the faces of other commuters for signs of things to come. They didn't seem like they were living an extraordinary day, but as the bus neared home, the bright pink lips on an elderly woman and the crisp swish of the parka on a school kid felt like small miracles, like a good life was happening. The bus drove across the landscape

I knew like the lines in my palms. The stretch of plazas, the wide roads grey with dirt-soaked snow and ice, and periodic pedestrians. I bit my lip to keep myself from crying.

We finally reached my stop, the stop on Birchmount where Ba had gotten off a million times, every week for years. I broke into a jog across the road towards home. Traffic was light at this time of the morning, and there were no cars in either direction, but I sprinted anyway, running lightly on tiptoes across the place on the road where Ba had died, hoping to touch it and avoid it at the same time.

A smattering of leftover plastic reindeers and Santas greeted me as I passed. The crabapple trees lining the streets were skeletal and had grown taller, a bit thicker. When Darwin was little and wanted to climb these trees, Ba had said he had to wait for both his and the trees' bodies to grow big enough. Time suddenly felt suspended. This was the street where I had learned to ride a bike. This was the spot where Sophia had punched a kid for stealing Darwin's lunch and made his nose bleed. This is where Sophia and I had sat and woven dandelion necklaces. My neck grew tight. We had wreathed Ma in bracelets, necklaces, even rings made of the bright yellow flower, and she had worn them until the flowers wilted and fell apart. She had said we were so clever to make such lovely things out of weed. There were so many good times like these with Ma — true, real times when we laughed and loved one another. All that had not been a lie. I remembered them now.

Finally, I reached our bungalow. The paint was peeling along the eavestrough and the curtains were drawn. I went up the front walk. The metal "25" on our mailbox still listed slightly to the left as it always had. I straightened it.

It felt awkward to ring the doorbell of my own home, but I was not sure it was mine anymore to just walk in. I pressed it, and heard the chimes, then footsteps. Not too fast, nor too slow. I measured the beats between the foot drops, trying to gauge whether they were excited or dreaded my coming.

Finally, Sophia opened the door. She was still as pretty as she ever was. She had cut her hair, and it reached her chin in layers. I was happy to see that she was wearing one of her *Flashdance* sweatshirts. She moved aside, expressionless.

"C'mon in," she gestured listlessly.

The first thing that hit me was the smell. Home always had this smell. I had never really considered it consciously, but as soon as I stepped in, I smelled all the meals that had ever been cooked, the familiar laundry detergent, the dusty rugs, and the scent of everyone I loved. I inhaled deeply.

"Don't just stand there. Take off your boots and coat," Sophia said. Her voice was flat. She wasn't going to let me off that easily. I slipped off my boots and unzipped my coat. From the corner of my eye, I saw a shadow in the hallway.

"Darwin?" I said gently.

He emerged, a fully grown person, almost taller than me. "Darwin?" I said again as if he were a ghost that might disappear. He walked towards me tentatively. His face was the same, perhaps more elongated. But the eyes, nose, mouth were all Darwin. I rushed at him. I didn't care if he was mad or wanted nothing to do with me. I needed to touch him.

He stood still as I tackled him and hugged him to me. After a moment, his arms reached around me and he hugged me back. I let out a sigh of relief then started to cry. Finally, I pulled away to look at him. He was smiling.

"I'm sorry, Darwin, I ... there's a lot I want to tell you, both of you..." I began. They didn't say anything, but something told me there would be lots of time to get into it all.

"Come on. You want something to eat?" Sophia said as she walked into the kitchen.

"I'm starving."

I followed them into the kitchen slowly, trying to recapture my old home on the way in. Everything was the same. How could it have just sat here like this all this time? I imagined the house without us, and it gave me a pang of sadness.

When I saw the table, my throat seized up again. In the centre was a plate of towering pancakes next to a bottle of maple syrup, some butter, and glasses of orange juice. It was set for three. They sat down, and then looked at me to join them. I pulled up a chair, and we picked up our forks and filled our plates like nothing had ever happened.

Darwin went first. "It happened in October. I was rehearsing with the symphony. It was Sibelius, and I had a solo. Cello. Anyway, me and this guy Marcel were rehearsing together late one night when suddenly, my fingers just stopped working. It was like they got mummified or something. I couldn't move them fast enough to catch the strings. But not only that, my brain shut off. The music was right in front of me on the stand, but I couldn't understand the notes anymore. It just stopped like that." He snapped his fingers. His voice was lower, having lost that ungainly squeak that had plagued him the year before.

"Mine disappeared more gradually," Sophia interjected. "I was giving a lecture in a grad seminar at McGill. I was explaining Cantor's theorem. I know, child's play, right?" I raised one eyebrow and smiled. "Anyway, I started working it out on the board, and I hear this student call out how I had made a mistake. That had never happened to me before. I'd never made a mistake. But he was right. Right there, smack in the middle of the proof, I had taken a wrong turn with the assumption of infinite numbers...." Sophia paused and saw that Darwin and I were blank. "Okay, okay. To simplify, I fucked it up. It was a stupid mistake. And that was the first time. Then, no errors for a few days, and suddenly, I messed up again. And again. It started happening pretty regularly, so Professor Gorky took me to a psychiatrist. I got a CAT scan, and everything looked normal. The only thing was, I'd lost my Gift."

"Then what happened to you two?"

Darwin said, "They took me to doctors too. I also got a CAT scan and a bunch of other stuff. Like, they made me do puzzles and take tests. And I had to talk to a therapist and tell him my dreams. Then, that was it. They sent me home."

"They did all that stuff with me too, then they sent me home," Sophia said.

"When? Where was Ma? Was she—"

"I got home in mid-October, and Darwin came soon after that. Ma was already in the hospital, so her friends came to check in on us. We've seen her...." Sophia started to scratch her arm. Trails of red welts ran up and down her skin.

"Yeah, but she's like Han Solo in the deep freeze. She's awake, but she's not there. Catatonic. That's what the doctors call it," Darwin finished for her. I could tell from their faces that it was bad. When Sophia got scared, she had a habit of twirling her hair with her fingers, and she was doing that now, furiously.

"Where's William?" I asked.

"Pssssh, William! He's gone. Once Ma got all *deen* all over again, he split. Couldn't handle it," Sophia said, with a scowl on her face. The image of William as an evil warlord vanished, and I recognized him for what he was: scared. In other words, human. I actually felt bad for the guy.

"What's happening now? What are you doing for money and stuff?"

"They didn't take away the money we had already earned. And Ba's estate money is still there. Since I'm not a minor anymore, I can get access to Ma's accounts because I'm her power of attorney. But there're these doctors who are still studying Darwin and me. We are still going to therapy and getting tested and whatnot. They're not sure what happened or if we'll get The Gifts back."

"Wow," was all I could say.

"Okay, your turn," Darwin said, interrupting my thoughts.

It struck me as utterly stupid to have to catch up these two people, my brother and sister, on the details of my life, as if we were on a blind date. But I had to start or we would not ever find our way back to normal. I took a breath, then said, "I live downtown. I'm working. At a community centre. I like it. It's with new immigrants. Um ... what else? I made a new friend. His name is Mouse. And...." I did not know what else to say. "I've missed you both very much."

"Are you coming home now?" Sophia asked me, a hint of the anger from the night before flickering in her voice. She had shoved the sleeves of her sweatshirt up to her biceps, and the scabs went all the way up, like healing chicken pox. It hurt me to see them.

I looked around at the plywood cabinets, the worn linoleum floors, the pea green stove that matched the pea green fridge. I nodded. "Of course I am," I whispered.

"Good," Darwin said, and for some reason, I felt as if I had passed a test.

After breakfast, Sophia watched music videos on MuchMusic, and Darwin played a video game while I toured the house. I lingered in Ma and Ba's bedroom, fingering the clothes that still hung in the closet. Perhaps Ma was in such a hurry when The Gifts came, that she had not bothered to put all these things away. Or maybe she had not been able to do it without us. I took out a suit of Ba's. He only had three that he had alternated for work. They were identical, except in different colours. He had bought them at Woolco at a "Buy one, get two more at half price" sale. This one was dark brown, double-breasted. The other one had been navy blue. That was the one he had died in. The third one was light grey. That was the one he was buried in. I brought the remaining suit up to my face, hoping to find Ba's scent. There was a faint hint of *Old Spice*, but that was all. I hung the suit back on the rail and took out one of Ma's dresses. It was her best dress, the one she saved for special church events. It was black with small red, purple, pink, and blue flowers printed on it, and the collar was edged in lace. I hung the dress back into the closet so it faced the brown suit. I laid down on their bed stripped of linen. The naked mattress felt cold against my body. The sounds of Darwin's game and Sophia's videos permeated the house. The Talking Heads' song "And She Was" played over the *chuuu chuuu* sounds of *Space Invaders*. The words drifted over me.

That night in the darkened bedroom, as I lay in bed on my side of the room, and Sophia lay in hers, she asked, "Miramar, were you ever jealous that Darwin and I got The Gifts and you didn't?"

I turned the question over before answering, "Yeah, I was."

Her breathing was even. "I thought so." She paused. "Is that why you left?"

"I don't know. Maybe it had to do with The Gifts. Mostly, it just had to do with me."

"You know, it wasn't all it was cracked up to be. The Gifts, I mean. I didn't choose mine. It chose me."

"What do you mean?"

"At first, it was great. Everyone treats you like you're hot shit. But then, they just expect you to be a superstar all the time, and they keep raising the bar. After a while, I was just a trained seal. To tell you the truth, there were moments when I wanted it all to end. For one thing, the stupid Gift meant I had no friends. I was like a freak show. Who wants to be friends with a freak show?"

"What about Iris?"

"Iris was nice. And I think she understood me, but a sixty-year-old woman wasn't going to hang out at the mall with me, ya know?"

"And all those boyfriends ... the Gorky's son, the deli man?" I said.

"I made them up."

"Why?" I was perplexed. I had been hooked, lined, and sinkered. I had even worried about her.

"I was bored."

"Geez, Sophia." I sighed. After considering it all, I could not blame her too much. "So you must have been glad when you lost your Gift, huh?"

"Not really. Mostly I was scared. Who was I if I didn't have my Gift? Where was I gonna go? You were all gone."

I had no answer for this. I sat up and reached for her.

"Sophia," I said, wishing she would sit up too and look me in the eye. "I am sorry. I will never leave you again." I held up my hand.

She waited a second then hooked her pinky with mine.

Chapter 32

Zhen knew all the herbs to be found in the woods. She recognized the roots that cooled the blood and the flowers that warmed it. She could cure water in the lungs by rubbing her concoctions to the chest. She made old woman Chu walk again with her specialty soup. But as talented as she was, and though there was much demand for her healing, Zhen had never found the remedy for a broken heart.

THE NEXT DAY, I went with Sophia and Darwin to see Ma. The psych ward at Scarborough General was different from the one downtown. It was older, with big cinder-block walls painted an institutional grey while the corridors were lit with fluorescent tubes. It was deathly quiet except for a constant drip, like maybe someone had not tightened the tap in a sink. The nurses did not seem to speak, only nodded at us. Sophia and Darwin led the way to Ma's room.

Ma lay in the hospital bed, slightly tipped up so she was partially sitting. Her gaze was fixed on the wall straight ahead of her. Her cheeks looked hollow, and the lines of her bones were prominent. Her lips were dry and the skin was flaking off. Much of her hair was completely white now. I went up beside her and whispered, "Ma?" She didn't even blink.

"It's me, Miramar. I'm back, Ma."

It felt risky to stand so close to her in case she startled and clawed at me with her hands. I wondered vaguely whether she was faking and now that I was this close, she would scream bloody murder at me for dropping out of school.

But she just sat there, staring at the grey wall. A tray was attached to her bed. Some untouched mound of chicken à la king and a pudding cup sat on a pink plastic plate.

"Who feeds her?" I asked Sophia and Darwin.

"The nurses eventually do it. They leave it for her in case she gets hungry and does it herself. She hasn't yet," Darwin answered.

Sophia sat down on the chair while Darwin perched himself on the edge of the bed. "What do you guys say to her when you come?"

"Nothing much. We just sit with her for a bit," Sophia murmured. The dripping water from down the hall now seemed deafening. Sophia's hands absently went to her sleeves. "Okay," I said, settling into the other chair. Ma's face and those stone eyes unnerved me. I studied her hands, the purple veins that popped up from her flesh. They looked like they belonged to someone else, someone ancient. I had been so angry at her. I had felt betrayed and lied to for all those years, all those supposedly miserable years she had spent with us in that house in Scarborough. As I sat in the room with its hums and tinny smells, I saw the bigger picture. If a lie included omission, then she had lied. I had thought she was happy. She had given up so much, almost everything that meant anything to her. She'd done it for us. It was the most precious unaddressed gift I had ever known. I saw it now, laid out here in her.

I didn't bother going back into town for my things; I called into work and they gave me time off for my "family crisis." I continued to see Ma every day. At first, it felt like penance. I was so sorry and had so much to make up for.

Some days, it was comforting to be close to her. Other days, I wanted to shake her and scream in her ear to break her out of this world she seemed to have succumbed to. I did not, of course. Instead, we waited and listened to the clock in her room count the seconds, minutes, and hours that marked the widening distance between us. With the nurse's help, I washed and combed her hair. I clipped her finger and toenails, and was surprised to see we shared the same feet: square, with the second toe longer than the big toe. Why had I not known this before? I had never touched my mother this much. Or at all, really. I imagined Ma having done all this for us for years and regretted not remembering how it felt to be cared for by her.

As the days passed, we fell into something of a routine. Darwin was being home-schooled because the Board of Education did not know what to do with ex-child geniuses, so until they could figure out another course of action, they were sending a tutor to the house every morning. Sophia had earned her doctorate in Mathematics while she still had her Gift, but since she couldn't do simple algebra now, McGill was considering stripping her of her title. Mainly, she sat at home and watched TV. Sophia and Darwin also had weekly meetings with a therapist who worked in the same building Ma was in.

One day, Sophia told me the therapist wanted to talk to me.

"Why?" I asked. I certainly did not have any Gifts to lose.

"I dunno. But she's nice. You'll like her," Sophia told me.

So the next week I found myself sitting in Dr. Fey's office, a room so unlike Ma's room just a few floors up. It had a large window that overlooked the ravine. Even as I was sitting on her couch, I could see the icy branches of the trees.

Dr. Fey followed my gaze. "Nice, eh? I think the best thing about this whole building is this window and the view." I liked this doctor. She had closely shorn black hair with spots of grey, and a pair of cat-eye glasses with small rhinestones at the corners. Her voice was smooth and warm, like honey.

"Yes, it's nice."

"So, you're probably wondering why I wanted to see you?"

I crossed my legs and waited.

"I've been talking to Darwin and Sophia for these past few months, and we've been trying to get to the bottom of why they seemed to have lost what you all call The Gifts."

I nodded.

"I was hoping that maybe you could fill in some blanks for me, so I can continue helping them." She took her glasses off. Her wide brown eyes had so much concern in them. I wondered if she had learned how to make that expression in school or whether she actually cared about people that much. "What do you think was the cause of The Gifts?"

I fumbled for something to say. Could I tell her what I really thought? Why not? If she thought I was crazy, at least I was in the right place. Ma and I could be roommates.

"My father died right before Sophia and Darwin got The Gifts. I think ... I think ... that maybe, he had something to do with it." There. I said it.

Dr. Fey leaned forward. "Go on."

"Darwin had this dream that Ba said he was going to take care of us. And then, a couple of days later, Darwin started playing the violin and piano and drums. Then it happened to Sophia right after."

"What about you? What happened to you?" This was the question I dreaded most. If Ba had given The Gifts to them, then why not also to me?

"Nothing."

"How did that make you feel, Miramar?"

"How did I feel? I don't know. It was pretty overwhelming." I decided right there I did not want to think anymore. I wanted to remove my head and pour it in the doctor's lap. Maybe she could sort it out, repair it and give it back to me and I would be good to go.

"Maybe ... maybe, I wasn't worthy of it," I stammered. My hands began to sweat.

"Really? But you seem like a good person. I mean, Darwin and Sophia think you're the best thing since sliced bread. And they said you were always the good kid, the one closest to your dad. Why would he leave you out?"

"I don't know," I replied. "I'll have to think about that."

"Good. I hope you do. That's all for today, Miramar. Would you come see me again sometime? I mean, to help me with Darwin and Sophia?" She stood up, smoothing her grey tweed skirt.

"Sure. I'm here every day to see Ma anyway." I also quickly got up.

"That's great. I'm always free around noon to two. Maybe we can have lunch sometime." She walked toward the door, putting her glasses back on as she did.

"I'd like that." I said it to be polite, because like she said, I had always been the good kid. But then as soon as I said it, I realized I meant it completely.

Chapter 33 ~

After ten years of battle, Kue made her way home. As she neared her village, she saw two figures approaching her. She ran to them, not believing that she was not alone in the world. Their faces had changed, their limbs grown longer, and they towered over her. But they recognized her immediately and called her Ga Jia — Big Sister.

THAT CHINESE NEW YEAR in February, with Ma still a stone figure in her room, Sophia, Darwin, and I went to Swiss Chalet. In a corner booth among cheerful families, we ordered the works: rotisserie chicken, hand-cut fries, and apple pie. It wasn't the elaborate meal we were used to having from Ma's kitchen, but we had made a promise to each other that we would be together, and here in this booth in this restaurant, we were. This fact was so singular and special it demoted all the other seasonal traditions to secondary. Besides, we loved Swiss Chalet. As kids, we had always begged to come here, but Ma had always scoffed that it was a major rip-off. "You want chicken? I make you chicken," Sophia imitated Ma. Darwin and I cracked up.

"Remember the year Ba brought us here when Ma went on that church trip to see the fall colours in Muskoka?" I reminded them.

"And Ba told us not to tell Ma!" Darwin chimed in. That year, the four of us had eaten our Swiss Chalet meal like we were committing a felony. It made the forbidden chicken even that much more delectable in our minds and stomachs.

"We had funny parents," Sophia said.

"Hey. Ma's still here," I interjected. We all fell silent.

"I don't mind just hanging around and waiting for Ma to wake up. Anyway, it beats being a musical prodigy," Darwin stated as he forked some coleslaw into his mouth.

"Really?" I was a little more surprised than I was when Sophia had told me she had not found her Gift to be all that. He had seemed to somehow embrace his life as a musical prodigy more personally.

"Hell, yeah," he continued. "When was the last time I got to spend so much time just being a kid?" He smiled shyly. "I also get to hang out with the two of you."

"Wow, Darwin. You actually like your icky sisters?" Sophia teased him.

"Yeah, you're all right."

"What about music, Dar?" I asked.

"I like music. I still want to play. In fact," he sighed and lowered his voice. "I actually think it might be coming back a little." He eyed us nervously. "But swear you won't tell anyone!"

"What?" Sophia and I both shrieked at the same time, and then, by habit, we yelled, "Jinx."

Darwin leaned in closer to us. "I'm just not sure what I want to do about it yet."

"Seriously, Darwin?" Sophia asked.

"Yah. I picked up my school violin yesterday and started to play. I can do it. It's coming back."

I was speechless. I could not believe he had not told us this before.

"But look. I want to make the decisions this time with what I want to do, okay? I don't want to go back to London. I don't want to be performing again. I need a break. And I think I want to start my own band. I like rock. Not so thrilled about classical anymore." He continued to eat, gnawing on a drumstick.

Sophia and I just stared at him. He was so mature. I was acquiring a new respect for my brother.

"That sounds pretty good, Darwin."

"Nothing's happening to me," Sophia said.

"But do you want it to?" I asked her.

She thought about it. "Not sure. If it did come back, I wish it would come back as something else. Not math. Maybe in fashion design or something." She studied her fork as she considered the possibilities.

"You probably don't have to wait for The Gifts to return for that, Sophia. You're pretty good at ripping apart your clothes and sewing them back together already," Darwin commented.

"This is true," I agreed.

"Hmmm," was all Sophia said.

All in all it was a wonderful dinner in many ways, reminiscent of our first time with Ba when the chicken was the juiciest I had ever had. But, despite having my siblings back and by my side, all the food, even the pie, tasted like nothing. Ma was still wasting away, alone, in her room.

Chapter 34 ⤙

There was one more thing Lian needed to do before she returned home to vanquish the enemies who had occupied her village. She travelled to the bamboo grove to visit the old sage. She had heard he had the secret that could unleash a thousand years of peace. When she got there, she only saw an ancient man who had grown roots and was melded to a tree. She asked for the secret, but he appeared to be sleeping. After much poking, he finally lifted his head and met her eyes. His were cloudy and blue with age. He took her hand and dropped thin air onto her palm, and said, "Here you go."

"What did you give me?" she demanded.

"You better figure that out yourself, little girl. Don't you know all Chinese fables end this way? Now, shoo. I need to get back to sleep. Damn tourists."

ON DAYS WHEN I WAS ALONE with Ma, I tried to keep up some level of chatter just so she could hear my voice. I told her how Sophia was planning to apply to fashion design school and seemed really excited, while Darwin had returned to school and was hanging out with all his old friends again. We had made some room in the basement for his Atari, so everyone could come over and have a place to hang out. He was a teenager, after all. I had never talked to her this much in my life, but even with all the news about my siblings, I ran out of easy things to say. There were, of course, other things I wanted to say. Like that I was sorry for leaving her. That I was beginning to understand some things. These sentiments did not come easily, but one day I forced myself. I stumbled with them but it got easier the more I talked. It would have been a nice touch, I thought, to do it in Cantonese, so I actually tried, even without having the right vocabulary. I took my time and stretched it out over many visits. I also did things I had always wanted to do but never had the chance to. I stroked her hair, touched her face. I tried to bring her back to me, to love her differently.

One afternoon, I took the elevator down to Dr. Fey's floor. I was hoping to bump into her, make it seem like a chance encounter. I did not see her then, so I began doing it every day at lunchtime. It took me a week, but one day, I caught her coming out of her office. There was something so elegant and competent about her, the way she dressed in luxurious knits and wools, wore clean perfume, and exuded an easygoing warmth.

I cruised by her as if I was on my way to somewhere.

"Hey, Miramar," she called after me.

I swivelled and feigned surprise. "Hi, Dr. Fey." I walked back to her door.

"What are you doing down here?"

"Um, just taking a walk. I was visiting Ma."

She smiled. "Wanna have that lunch?"

"Sure."

And so, that was how it started. Each Tuesday and Thursday, while Dr. Fey ate a sandwich in the cafeteria, I told her stories about Ba, Ma, Sophia, Darwin, and me. And *kung fu*. And Mouse. Dr. Fey laughed at my stories. She said I had a gift for storytelling. Mouse would've been proud on my behalf. I vaguely let myself wonder if anything would ever happen to our scripts.

"What are you going to do about this young man, Mouse?" she asked me one day between bites of her tuna sandwich.

"I don't know. What should I do?"

"Do you like him? Like, really *like* him?" she teased.

"Yeah. I do." I smiled at the thought of Mouse and his antics. "I love him." There, I had said it, and saying it out loud made me realize how true and simple it was.

"Well, that's the answer to your question then."

If only everything were that easy. I could only deal with one thing at a time. First, I had to wait for Ma to do something, anything. Until then, I could not talk to Mouse. I did not have enough room in my body left for more than one complication at a time. But I missed him. I wanted to see his smile, to hear his loud laugh. As much as I assumed we lived exclusively in make-believe, it occurred to me that Mouse was the most real thing that had happened to me since Ba died.

I had been staying in Scarborough for three weeks when Dr. Fey presented me with a theory. We were in the cafeteria and it was humming with people. I had to lean in to hear her. "Perhaps the grief of losing your father caused some kind of neurological process in Sophia and Darwin. Some tapping of a certain part of their neocortex resulting in their sudden extraordinary talents."

I considered this. "But why did they lose The Gifts? And at about the same time? What, they got over their grief, just like that?" I asked.

"Have you?" She sipped her tea.

"No. I'll never get over it." Since coming home, I missed Ba more than ever.

"I didn't think so. I don't think they will either. But maybe something changed. Some shift. Maybe they're ready to cope with their loss without The Gifts now."

"I'm not sure what you mean," I said.

"The human spirit is a resilient thing. It has the will to do whatever it takes to survive, even thrive, under the most horrendous circumstances. Perhaps your sister and brother needed The Gifts. Temporarily. Until they were able to let them go and live life without your father."

"And me?"

"You, Miramar, seem to be resourceful enough without The Gifts." She considered this for a moment. "Or," she smiled, "your Ba really was responsible for The Gifts, and he's saving one for you."

"That's not a very scientific explanation." I arched my eyebrows at her.

"I know." She nudged me with her elbow. "Cool, eh?" She paused. "There's something else I need to tell you. You know how I asked you to see me that first time, to help me with Sophia and Darwin?"

I nodded.

"Well, it was actually Sophia and Darwin's idea. They thought maybe I could help you."

I jerked back in my chair.

"They thought it would be good for you to have someone to talk to." She looked at me expectantly.

"Really?" I sat way back in my chair. I thought I was back to help them, but here they were trying to help me. I imagined how I must have seemed to them then, and yup, I probably did come across as pretty fucked up.

"Yes. What do you think about that?"

"I don't know. What do *you* think about that?" I asked. Maybe I actually did need some major help of the psychiatric kind.

"I think, as a professional and all, that you're okay, kid." She gave me a wink and took a big bite of her sandwich.

"And Ma? What about Ma?" I asked.

Dr. Fey chewed thoughtfully and considered my question. "That remains to be seen, Miramar. I think your Ma has a long way to travel to come back. Hopefully, she's making her way."

I nodded. It seemed Ma's way was to finally give herself the solitude she needed to regroup, to let go of what she knew and loved and missed so badly; our way was to screw up and fall down and get back up and try again. All any of us wanted was to get back to normal, but normal was over. There was no normal, and all we had was now. I did not know what it was, this current state, and suspected it would be a long haul before we got to where we were supposed to go.

Chapter 35 ~~

In the final challenge, it would take all of them to come together — the servant girl, the undercover princess, the bandit queen, the shepherdess, the blind girl, the woman warrior, the assassin. The women gathered in a circle and took up their kung fu stances and waited. Their ribbons flew like flags from their hair, their limbs, their swords, and their staffs. They would have to use all their powers to change fate and redetermine their destiny. The universe was held in a precarious balance between what was right and what was to be.

ONE NIGHT AFTER MIDNIGHT, the phone rang. I groped for my glasses on the night table, stumbled out of bed, and hurried to the kitchen phone.

"Hello?"

"I'm calling from Scarborough General. Is this Ga Bo Woo's daughter?"

My legs turned weak. Oh my God, please do not let her be dead, I thought to myself, please.

"Mrs. Woo is not in her bed. Is she with you?" The person at the other end struggled to sound professional even though I could hear the panic in her voice.

I gripped the receiver. "No. I just saw her. I fed her dinner. She was the same as always. Are you sure you're talking about my mother? Room 921?"

"Yes, dear. I'm sorry, no need to be concerned. She must be around here somewhere. We do hourly check-ins with the patients, but in between that time, she must have gotten out of bed—"

"I'll be right there." I hung up and yelled, "Sophia, Darwin! Get up. Ma's missing!" Then I ran back to the bedroom and flicked the light switch on, looking for clothes. Sophia sat up and shook her head of sleep.

"What's going on?"

"Get dressed. Ma's missing." She snapped awake and joined me on the floor, looking through our piles of clothes for something to put on. Darwin ran into the room, already dressed.

"Let's go, let's go!" he cried.

We took a taxi to the hospital. Now that it was March, the worst of winter was behind us. The asphalt was wet with the thawing snow. We drove through the dark, empty streets. I held Darwin and Sophia's hands in mine. The woman on the phone had assured me Ma was likely close by, that they would find her, that maybe she was having a stroll in the halls, but I knew that something was terribly wrong.

"She's gone. We searched everywhere," the doctor in charge of the night shift told us. My stomach dropped. I had hoped I was just being dramatic, that my sense of impending doom was stupid. "We have security looking all over the building for her. She couldn't have gone far. She's only in her hospital gown."

We were told to wait. I couldn't bear it. Sophia, Darwin, and I rode up and down the escalator, checking on every floor. Finally, I was convinced she simply was not there.

"Miramar, we have to do something!" Sophia's teeth were chattering.

"I know, I know. Let me think." There was only one person in the world I could call. I looked at a clock; it was two-thirty a.m. Maybe Mouse was still at Dusk. I ran to the pay phone in the waiting room, called Directory Assistance and got connected to the bar's line.

"Allo?" I heard people and music. The place was still going strong.

"Is Mouse there, please."

"Mouse. Hold up." I heard muffled sounds and then someone yelling, "Mouse, phone's for you." I did not know how to feel: happy, nervous, grateful? I sighed, relief rushing through my body.

"Wai?" Mouse answered.

"Mouse. It's me, Miramar. I need your help."

"Miramar? Where are you? What's going on?"

"Can you get a car? My Ma is missing."

"Give me the address. I'll be there in twenty minutes."

We hung up and it occurred to me that whether I was asking him to go around the block or journey to another country, when Mouse said he would be here in twenty minutes, I completely believed him.

Mouse and I drove around the area surrounding the hospital. We crawled at a snail's pace through the residential streets with a flashlight Mouse brought from the bar. Sophia and Darwin remained at the hospital in case someone found her. At every pay phone, I stopped to check in. She was nowhere. She had vanished, like vapour.

We were in a beat-up Ford Escort that had holes in the floor, which flooded us with the cool air outside and the loud rumble of the engine. Bull, the owner of Dusk, lent it to Mouse.

"Thanks for coming so quickly," I said while we drove.

"No problem. You've never asked me for help before, ya know."

I stared straight ahead.

"It's nice," he said as he scanned the streets.

We kept our eyes on the sidewalks, searching every crevice and shadow. Sometimes, cats appeared out of the darkness, flushed out of hiding by our roving flashlight. Each street seemed like a carbon copy of the other and soon we felt as if we had gone down the same street twice.

We widened our circumference from the hospital, making larger loops through the suburban terrain. Finally, we were getting closer to my neighbourhood. At the next plaza, we stopped so I could call Sophia and Darwin at the hospital again. They still hadn't found Ma. Mouse and I continued our drive until I began to direct him toward my house.

I wasn't sure if it was instinct, but my internal compass pressed me home. The sun was already rising by the time we turned the corner onto my block. The light hit the houses, scattering and breaking up the dark. Traffic had already started picking up, and cars collected in the lanes, preparing to merge onto the highway for the long commute to work. "Wait, no, turn around," I said, pointing. It hit me. Before we went back to the bungalow, there was one place I had to check first.

I was right. Ma was standing in the exact spot where Ba had died, in the middle of two opposing rivers of traffic. I pointed to her, and Mouse screeched the car over to the side of the road and put on the emergency lights. I looked at Mouse for some indication of what to do, but he looked terrified, his face pale and his eyes wide. I got out of the car, drivers behind us honking their horns.

Ma stood with both her feet on the solid white line, the division between the eastbound and westbound lanes, her face thoughtful, as though she were a tightrope walker. She only had on her hospital gown and a terrycloth bathrobe over it. Her calves were blotched with red, and her hospital slippers were wet and dark with mud. The river of cars sprayed water all around her.

I ran to the curb closest to her and yelled.

Ma turned her head toward the sound of my voice. She smiled a small smile and pointed at the two lanes of traffic. The cars sped past her, oblivious. "Which way, *nui*? East? Back to Hong Kong? Back to my parents? Back to my home? Shall I go back?" she cried in Cantonese. Her voice was high and reedy like a child's.

Then, turning again, she pointed toward the other two lanes. "Or should I go that way? Is that the right way? West? Maybe we haven't arrived yet." She spoke and weaved dangerously forward and backward slowly, as if in a dream.

"Please, Ma. Don't move. I'm coming to get you!" I was shaking violently. "I'm sorry. For everything. Please, Ma. I need you. I need you." My voice cracked.

When I said those words, I knew them to be truer than ever. I needed her.

"Which direction, Miramar? Which way did Ba go? I don't remember. Tell me. I want to go to him."

I stood, frozen on the curb watching her helplessly. She wrung her hands and started to scream, "*Nui, nui,* where is he? Where is Ba?"

Hearing Ma wanting to join Ba made something explode in me — all my grief over Ba, all my worry for Sophia and Darwin and Ma, and all my love too. The memory of what love had been like when Ba was alive. I felt an enormous force blast from my body and then, suddenly, everything came to a complete halt. The moving landscape froze. The cars, the sound, the wind lashing my hair all over my face — all of it stopped. There was just stillness. The air was so thick I could feel it closing around me like an embrace. I saw the faces of the drivers, their eyes like stones. I saw a baby in the backseat, his mouth still open in the middle of a wail, and his mother's face, contorted in frustration. I looked back at the car and saw Mouse, his eyes still wide and fixed on me. And Ma. She was standing with her feet on the line, her eyes downcast. I stepped between the cars to reach her. And then, there was Ba, standing beside her. He looked exactly as I remembered, his briefcase in one hand, his other hand beckoning me to come closer. I reached them, and he stroked me on the cheek and then guided my hand to Ma's. Hers was icy and pointy with bones. Then he was gone.

Around us, the vehicles snapped back into motion, the sounds of their engines drowning out my thoughts. What had just happened? Ma's hand was freezing against my warm one. She slowly lifted her vacant eyes. "*Nui?*" she whispered.

"Just my hands, Ma. Just my hands now," I said softly.

With my other hand, I extended it to signal to the cars to stop. They immediately halted, as if we had suddenly materialized and were for the first time, visible. Gently, I led my mother back to the curb. Once there, we collapsed into an embrace. I cried into her hair, my legs weak, and let her comfort me. She patted my back, rubbing circles into my skin. "Don't cry, *nui nui*. It's okay. Ma's here now. Don't cry."

Chapter 36 ~~

AFTER BRINGING MA HOME, Mouse went to collect Sophia and Darwin from the hospital. A doctor came with them to check on Ma. Thankfully, she was fine. She was cold, she was tired, and still frail, but otherwise she was in good form. The first thing she said to me after I got her in some dry clothes and tucked her into bed was, "*Nui,* I'm hungry."

I made her my specialty — instant noodles with a slice of ham and fried eggs. This was how Sophia and Darwin found her, slurping noodles like she hadn't eaten in years.

Sophia ran right to her, burying her head in her chest and clutching at Ma's covers. "I'm so sorry, Ma. I'll try to be better. I swear."

Ma set her bowl down on the bed and reached with her hands to stroke Sophia's head. "*Tsaw nui,* shhhh. Okay, now. I'm okay."

Darwin hung back by the door until Ma looked up and reached her other hand out to him. He joined her on the bed too and the three of them clung to each other.

Later in the day, they all took a much-needed nap. I lay down too, but sleep did not come. Perhaps it was the adrenaline of the night before, and the extraordinary event on the road with Ma. I went out to the living room where Mouse was sitting quietly.

He sat up, his face suddenly energized. "*Lang lui,* it was incredible. One second you were on the curb, calling out to your Ma, and the next, you were right there with her. You actually did it! You ground the axis of the earth to a stop!" He jumped up on the couch with excitement.

"Shhhh! Everyone's sleeping."

"Oh, sorry!" He stepped back on the floor. It was strange to see him in our living room, as if two worlds were being superimposed onto each other.

"I don't think I did it alone. I just think that for once I was in the right place, at the right time." I didn't want to tell him about seeing Ba. It was too precious. Some things could not be explained with words. What I knew to be true was wondrous, and it all happened. Just like Sophia and Darwin's Gifts, what happened out there on the road was as real as anything else in the world. It wasn't the explanations or reasons that mattered. It was that they happened at all.

Outside, it began to rain, a light drizzly mist that seemed to signal spring was on its way.

"Hey, *lang lui,* listen. About that night..." Mouse had moved to Ba's old chair while I sat on the carpet.

"Mouse, I'm sorry."

"No, you were right about a lot of things. I mean, not everything, in case you think you're a smartass."

I kicked his feet playfully. "Okay, so tell me what I was wrong about."

"I do live in my own world. Whether you think it's nuts or not, I created it and ... it's mine."

"I had no right to disrespect how you live."

"Yeah. Okay, apology accepted," he said, shrugging. "If there was one in there."

"Okay, so tell me where I was right."

"Where you were right, Missy Woo, is that there are parts of myself that I left behind. Maybe it's time to go back and get 'em. I mean, even the *kung fu* heroes have a past right? Even though they have to leave it behind, the past is still who they are."

"Go on."

"So, this is what I'm gonna tell ya." He sat back on Ba's recliner and stretched out. "Here's another story. About a guy name Arthur Ga Yee Chow."

He paused, looking at the popcorn ceiling. I felt a thrill happening; he was going to tell me the truth. The real story. "Ol' Arty was born in Duckbill in the Prairies. His Ba was the owner of the Glowing Lights Chinese and Canadian Food Emporium. He had tagged 'emporium' on the end because he thought it sounded classy. So, Arty grew up in the kitchen, tied to his Ma's back while she churned out everything from chicken balls and egg rolls to grilled cheese and hot beef sandwiches smothered in gravy while Dad gave the customers his best Chinaman: *Yessy, boss. Okaeey, Boss. You the Boss!*"

Mouse's eyes were still pointed upward, but he did not have the familiar dreamy look he got when he told stories. There was a softening in his face. He looked like a child.

"They were the only Chinese family in Duckbill. Let's just say, aside from the *chop suey*, they were not a big hit in the local community."

He grew silent. I lay down on the carpet, also looking at the ceiling, recognizing a light brown stain where years ago, Darwin had thrown Sophia's dish of chocolate ice cream when she would not let him have the TV converter.

I thought about all the stories Mouse had told me, realizing for once, that for every one, there was one he had never told. It was the one that did not end with the hero's victory, the exaltation, the triumphant recognition of his greatness. I imagined a kid named Arthur, small as a mouse, in some tiny prairie place, inventing his future.

His eyes were closed, and he nodded in memory. "An overactive imagination and a whole shitload of *kung fu* movies saved Arty's ass. He may not have known who he was, but he knew who he wanted to become."

"Where are your parents, Mouse?"

"Ma died. Cancer. It was quick. Dad went back to the four villages. 'Nothing left here,' he said. I could have gone, but…" he stopped. He looked a little forlorn.

I stood up and scooted him over so I could squeeze into Ba's La-Z-Boy recliner with him. "I think I would really like this Arthur guy. We have a lot in common," I said, taking his hand in mine.

I packed all my things from my apartment and moved back into the house in Scarborough. It was not going to be permanent, but for now, it was where I wanted to be. I kept my job at the community centre. I figured I was honing the skills I needed to be a real live woman warrior. They might not have been legitimate skills I could write in my CV: "Can do phone impersonations of government officials and lawyers," but I was helping. And Ma had always said I should be helpful.

Together we settled back into our quiet suburban life. Spring was coming. I smelled it in the damp crush of earth every time I took a step. Soon, the neighbourhood crabapple trees would blossom, lightening the dull grey street with their sprays of pink and white. The days would get longer, and the kids would play baseball on the street again.

Sophia had gotten accepted at a fashion design program at George Brown College downtown. She was already at work on her first collection, which she named "Geometry." Surprisingly, she decided she was over ripped sweatshirts and instead went heavy on shoulder pads and cinched waists — very Joan Collins from *Dynasty*. Afternoons were when she and Ma would make tea and sit together at the kitchen table, just like when Sophia was little, drawing ideas and poring over fabric samples.

Darwin's Gift was still coming in steadily, which he kept under wraps. He had gotten a glimpse of what being a grown-up meant, and he was smart enough to hold it back for as long as he could. Meanwhile, he found some kids from school to form a garage band. They named it Skywalker.

I took over all the finances and set us on a budget. Between the money we had saved from Darwin and Sophia's earnings, Ba's estate, and my income, we were going to be fine. Darwin was also confident that if need be, he could cut an album with Skywalker that he was certain would go double platinum in a matter of weeks. This would have sounded like hot air from anyone else, but I had heard them practicing, and I had to admit they were pretty great. Mouse said he would get them a gig at Dusk just to start out. When they were old enough to be allowed into a bar, of course.

Once she was strong enough, Ma went back to church and started playing *mah jong* again. We fought less, laughed more. Ba would have been proud of us.

I still missed him, but the missing came to me in different colours. Sophia, Darwin, Ma, and I began talking about him again, bringing Ba back into the house like the first warm breeze of the season. Sometimes, we would remember a funny story, and what began with laughter would occasionally turn to tears. And sometimes, what began as tears turned to laughter. There were days when the pain returned with all its sharp blades, but those days passed, became new ones. Ba was gone, but he was not gone.

While all the men go off to war to seek revenge, honour, and all those glorious things, it was the women who kept the clans together. Without them, there was no return.

Yes, but Ba, I think the women were also out there — in the battlefields, in the woods, in the hills. The women had quests too. But they came home because they wanted their families to be together again.

There were still boxes in the basement of his things that Ma's friends had packed for us. They stayed there waiting to be released again. That day had not arrived yet, but there was still time for all of that. I packed away all the "Dormant" files and set them in a box beside Ba's boxes. I didn't feel a need to read them anymore. I whispered their names one more time — Janeanne, Lee, Theresa, and Daniel. I wished each of these people who had felt like my friends, peace.

Two weeks after Ma's return, we sat down to a real Chinese New Year Dinner. We were late, but we had made it. Ma took her time, cooking for two days, and letting us help. In the end, we made the most memorable meal in the history of the Woo family: braised beef, steamed whitefish, stewed melon and shiitake mushrooms, fiery-hot jumbo shrimp, a slow-cooked soup, roast duck, and mussels in black bean sauce. To top it all off, Sophia and I made our traditional potato and fruit salad with generous mounds of mayonnaise.

Ma invited everyone: the church ladies, the neighbours, Dr. Fey, and even William K.C. Koo, who stood nervously to one side. I went over to him and handed him a can of Coke. "Hi, William."

"Hello, Miramar." I gave him the opportunity to squirm in the uncomfortable silence that followed.

"Miramar. I'm sorry I didn't take care of your mother." I regarded his face; his eyes were actually tearing up.

"William, you can only do what you are prepared to do. I've been learning that. And I think Ma's okay." We both looked over at her, as she scrambled between wok and oven, kitchen to dining room, asking each person if he was enjoying the food as she flew by.

"Well, thank you for understanding," he replied. He squinched his face then looked at me. "Do you think she hates me?" he asked.

"Hate you? No. She invited you here, didn't she? Give her some time." I watched his eyes follow Ma's frantic movements around the kitchen and realized that he really loved her.

"Go on, get something to eat before Ma yells at you for

having an empty plate." I smiled at him, and surprised myself that it felt genuine.

Mouse came too. He had been dropping in a few days a week, driving his boss' broken down Ford or taking the long ride on public transit. Ma seemed to like him.

"He's a bit, *hei mong mong*," she remarked to me. This meant he had his heads in the clouds, or in the fog, as the direct translation went. But she liked him. I could tell. He was ever the proper Chinese boy, never failing to compliment her on her fine cooking, even rolling up his sleeves to help. She was impressed with his way around a wok.

"*Wah, lo sui sek dut tsu yeh!*" The mouse can cook!

I watched him as he helped Ma ladle out the soup for all the guests. I was not sure what was going to happen between Mouse and me, but it was okay to not know the end before the story even really got started.

Acknowledgements

I am in deep gratitude to the wondrous women who have helped me learn what it means to be at once displaced and to occupy many spaces. I learned from them that voices are never singular but a chorus. Heartfelt thanks to Karen B. K. Chan, Eve Haque, Simone Browne, Nupur Gogia, Andrea Fatona, Judith Nicholson, May Lui, Davina Bhandar, Nira Elgueta, Vannina Sztainbok, Denise Hui and Tola Ajao.

I also want to acknowledge those friends who have supported my writing of this novel with enthusiasm, and especially to those who read early drafts. Deep appreciation to Lynn Caldwell, Catherine Burwell, Jen Parker, Estelle Anderson, Frances Miller, Kathy Liddle, Sarah Couture-McPhail, Cherie Lunau Jokisch and Cathy Bennett. I offer thanks to Farzana Doctor who is an inspiration and has considered me a sister writer before this novel even began. I have immense respect and love for Jenna Kalinsky, my teacher, my mentor, my editor and a great friend. This novel would not have been written without her holding my hand and sharing her keen passion for the craft. I am indebted to Luciana Ricciutelli and Inanna Publications for taking a chance on this story, and their commitment to publishing women writers.

My appreciation to my families — the Leungs and the Archdekins — for believing in my fortitude and pre-ordering books to give to their friends. My dogs, Kuro and Bella, are the best companions for a writer who values solitude but still needs a good walk and a wet kiss once in awhile.

Lastly, I give thanks to Andrew Archdekin who provides me with a soft place to land, and Fenn Archdekin-Leung who calls me home. Always.

Photo: Taralea Cutler

Carrianne K.Y. Leung is a fiction writer, educator, and business owner. She holds a Ph.D. in Sociology and Equity Studies from OISE/University of Toronto and works at OCAD University. Carrianne is also the co-owner of Multiple Organics. She, her partner, their son, and two dogs live in the west-end of Toronto.